BRON


*The Blades of Janus*
PACK
PROGENITOR


*The Forbidden Knights*
FORBIDDEN INSTINCT


*The Summer Park Psychics*
WANDERING SOUL
WHISPERING HEARTS
LINGERING TOUCH
THE SUMMER PARK PSYCHICS OMNIBUS


Other Works
CRAFTING A WRITER'S LIFE: Building a Foundation


*Coming Soon*


*Court of the Summer Fae*
The Huntsman
The Green Man
The Big Bad Wolf


*Cygnian 7*
TARN
ROM

# The Oak King

Court of the Springtime Fae
Book Three

*Cassandra Chandler*

# Copyright Page

This book is pure fiction. All characters, places, names, and events are products of the author's imagination or used solely in a fictitious manner. Any resemblance to any people, places, things, or events that have ever existed or will ever exist is entirely coincidental.

The Oak King
Court of the Springtime Fae, Book Three
Copyright © 2024 by Cassandra Chandler
Print ISBN: 978-1-945702-11-2
Digital ISBN: 978-1-945702-10-5

First eBook edition: May 2024
First print edition: May 2024
10 9 8 7 6 5 4 3 2 1

cassandra-chandler.com
P.O. Box 91
Mission, Kansas 66201

# Dedication

For Traci, who works her own magic on plants.

*Don't miss out on any of the magic.*
*Subscribe to Cassandra Chandler's newsletter at*
*cassandra-chandler.com!*

# Chapter One

The quiet murmur of conversation surrounded Emma as she sat in one of the best restaurants in Crystal Hollow. Well, one of the fanciest, at least. She already knew how to cook any dish on the menu. In reality, when it came to having someone cook for *her*, she'd be happier with a stack of pancakes and bacon, especially since it was early enough to call this a late brunch. This place was particularly egregious to her because she had worked with half the staff. They catered to the most pretentious clientele possible and were absolutely fine with elitism as long as they could turn a nice profit.

She did not want to be here. Places like this had driven her to abandon her successful career as a high-end chef and open her own catering business instead. Try to, at least. She was still struggling to get her business off the ground. And now, this…

She wriggled in her seat, adjusting the strap of the amethyst-purple sundress she was wearing. The vibrant color brought out the rich golden undertones of Emma's brown skin more effectively than the pale lavender dress that her best friend, Hayden, had encouraged her to wear at first. Emma didn't care if they were 'spring colors.' She didn't give a damn about impressing this guy. She did care about Hayden, so Emma had at least gone along with wearing the diamond and amethyst necklace that Hayden had insisted she wear, as well as a set of teardrop diamond earrings with amethysts at their center and several matching rings—none of which happened to be on the ring finger of her left hand.

Emma curled her hand into a fist and gently pounded the table, her nerves getting the better of her. A man at a nearby table glanced at her uneasily. She smiled at him and straightened her fork in its place setting.

"I would rather be anywhere than here," she muttered.

Apparently, so would her blind date. He was already ten minutes late. Emma was in no hurry to meet him. She had dragged her feet for the last two weeks while she 'learned the basics' of her new situation, but she couldn't put it off any longer, no matter how much she wanted to.

The pattering beat of her heart made her head ache. Her palms were coated in a fine sheen of sweat. Normally, she was as cool as cucumber water on blind dates. She knew what she wanted and wasn't afraid to communicate that. She also knew what she *didn't* want, and being here was close to the top of that list. However, Hayden had been adamant that this meeting needed to happen if Emma was ever going to get her life back. Emma didn't feel like she had much choice in the matter.

How did you say 'no' to a date with the Oak King?

Her stomach clenched. At this rate, she wouldn't be able to force anything down. Sharing a meal with a member of the High Fae wasn't something she ever thought she'd do. She hadn't let herself believe that fairies were real since she was a child. Ugly memories rose to the surface of her mind—memories she was usually adept at shoving back in place. Pleasant ones came with them. Those were even worse.

She would not be tricked again.

When Emma had come out of a magical trance two weeks ago at an event she was catering, Hayden had introduced Emma to Jack-freaking-Frost. Emma had been terrified to realize they'd all been swept into a fairytale. The stories were one thing, but Emma knew first-hand that they did not end well for humans. Mortals and Fae were not meant to mix. Then Hayden had dropped the bombshell. Finn, the guy they'd been working with for the event, was also an elf. The two of them were in love, and Finn had already altered Hayden and made her one of the Fae. Jack Frost had hooked up with Ava, so now both of Emma's best friends were *dating* elves.

At least they weren't 'kinda sorta married' to one, as she was.

Emma stretched out her left hand again, staring at the bare patch of skin on her ring finger. How the hell was she going to get out of this? And what could she do for her friends, who didn't know enough to be scared?

She had spent every free moment during the last two weeks going through all the books she had about the Fae, studying the Oak King and his counterpart, the Holly King. Both ruled over the Wheel of the Year. The Holly King oversaw the months where the nights were longer than the days—the dark half of the year. The Oak King ruled over the light half. Rather, the Oak King *and Emma*.

That was the only thing keeping her from utter panic. She had been infused with half of the power of the Wheel of the Year, making her a formidable opponent for any Fae who might think about pissing her off. Finn had been instructing both Emma and Hayden on how to use their new magic when Emma wasn't studying. She was more interested in controlling it just long enough to get rid of it safely.

She rubbed her forehead, trying to get her headache to go away. Suddenly being flooded with unimaginable magical power was doing a number on her. Or maybe it was just the stress of being dragged into this nightmare. It was almost as bad as the mind-twisting knowledge that somehow in all of this mess the Oak King had made her the Queen of the Springtime Fae. She still didn't understand why.

She didn't need to understand. She just had to get out of it. Fairies were not to be trusted. The fairytales she'd grown up on were clear about that. And if her own experience was to be believed... Emma shoved the memories away again before they could resurface completely. Maybe Ava and Hayden thought they had found themselves two exceptions to that rule, but they were a long ways off from their own 'happily-ever-afters.' Emma didn't trust any of the Fae.

A man entered the restaurant, wearing a dark suit, crisp white shirt, and silk tie. He was tall and lean, just as Ava and Hayden's Fae boyfriends were. There was a reason Emma and Ava had taken to calling Finn 'Prince Charming.' This guy's dark hair was cut short on the sides and longer on top. His features were striking, something she might see in a fashion magazine. Emma pinched her lips together, as if she might let slip thoughts she didn't want anyone else to hear.

*Not. My. Type.*

Not that anyone had bothered to ask her what her type was. Or even if she wanted to be the freaking Queen of the Springtime Court. No, the Oak King had just decided for her. Had *claimed* her as his queen. Emma was going to have some very choice words for him on that matter when he arrived. Words he probably would not like.

A breeze picked up around her, strong enough to make the flowers in the centerpiece of the table spin in their vase. Emma took a deep breath and let it out through pursed lips, counting back from five. By the time she reached one, the wind was gone.

She had to be careful of her emotions now that she had magic—magic that she was going to use to let every Fae that thought of making mischief for her and her friends know that they had picked the wrong mortals to mess with. Her lips twitched into a brief snarl. She was no one's to claim.

An older man at a nearby table stared at her, his eyes wide. This wasn't the time or place to lose control. Emma coughed into her hand while she schooled her expression, then gave him a patronizing smile and batted her eyelashes at him.

After he'd turned back around in his seat, she murmured, "Why the hell am I even doing this?"

The man she'd seen enter waved at someone across the room. Emma watched his progress weaving among the tables. He smiled as he made his way toward an equally gorgeous man who greeted him with a kiss on the cheek.

"Okay," Emma muttered. "I guess I'm not his type, either."

She turned back around in her chair just in time to see another man enter. He was so tall, he had to duck to keep his tawny brown hair from brushing the top of the archway between the dining room and the bar. A server slid past him and had to turn entirely sideways to fit through the space left over from the guest's massive shoulders. He wore a pale green, three-piece suit over a mint shirt, with a deep golden tie at his throat. He hooked a thick finger under the collar of his shirt as if to loosen it, but froze, grimacing as he left it be. He let his huge arm drop back to his side, his hands in fists.

Now this one—*this one*—was her type.

He scanned the room and their eyes locked. His scowl became a bit less pronounced, but his eyebrows lowered over his jade-green eyes, his focus fixated upon her. Shivers skittered up and down her spine, goosebumps rising on her arms. Her mind was immediately flooded with imaginative examples of just what the two of them could get up to if given the right opportunity. Which this was not.

Why did she have to meet this absolutely perfect example of a man when she was supposed to be having lunch with the Oak King? The man started making his way toward her, occasionally nudging aside people in their chairs to give him enough space to walk through the dining room.

Emma couldn't keep herself from grinning. She knew she shouldn't. She shouldn't even have made eye contact with this guy. Now she was going to have to find a way to let him down easy as quickly as possible. Who knew what the Oak King would do if he saw them together when he arrived. Maybe she could get this guy's number really discreetly…

He stopped right next to her table, looking profoundly

uncomfortable. He craned his neck to one side, then the other, a loud cracking sound coming from it with each movement. His hands kept flexing and curling alternately at his sides as he glanced around the room, then back to her, then back to the room, his mouth opening and closing as if he didn't know what to say.

"Hi," she said.

He froze, staring at her through narrowed eyes. "Hello."

"I'm Emma." She smiled at him, leaning forward on her elbows while playing with the strand of diamonds at her décolletage.

"Lachlan," he said, seeming relieved. He pulled out a chair and sat across from her.

"I'm actually meeting someone."

"I know." He leaned back in his chair and stared at her.

"Wait, you're not…"

"The Oak King?" he said. "I am."

This? This exquisite example of a man was her 'husband?' If it weren't for the impossible circumstances surrounding them, she would have been thrilled to hook up with him. Knowing what he was, how he had transformed her life into chaos…

'Thrilled' was not the right word. But she was certain she'd come up with a few choice ones throughout their blind date. She just had to be careful she didn't mess up her chance to get out of all this in one piece.

# Chapter Two

"Great." Emma leaned back, mirroring his posture. Her smile immediately morphed into a frown.

"You looked a lot happier to see me a moment ago," Lachlan said.

"I didn't know you were the Fae douchebag who upturned my life a moment ago."

His lips twitched at the corners. "I've been called many things in my long existence, but that one is new."

"Believe me, it's well-earned."

"The Holly King is the one who put half the power of the Wheel of the Year in you."

"And why did he do that? Because you claimed me as your queen."

"Would you rather I had left you unclaimed? An outsider surrounded by capricious Fae?"

"As opposed to you, who is so much more steadfast?"

"I am, actually."

She snorted and crossed her arms over her chest. Lachlan's eyes were drawn to the movement, and he noticed the necklace she was wearing. The same one that the Holly King had placed on her when he had split the power of the Wheel of the Year, accessorizing her for the part. She even had the rings and earrings on. For some reason, seeing her wearing the jewelry that the Holly King had created for her rankled Lachlan.

"Funny that you seem so angry with me for trying to protect you, but you have no problem wearing the gifts of the guy responsible for making you well and truly stuck in this position," he said.

"What are you talking about?"

He nodded toward her, staring at the necklace. "The jewelry. It was part of the ensemble the Holly King created for you when he infused you with the magic."

"I thought you did that."

"Are you kidding?" Lachlan snorted. "Did you see the dress he made for you? Queen of the Springtime Court or not, I would never put you in pastels. They don't suit you."

"I don't know whether to be flattered or insulted."

"How about neither? I'm just stating facts."

One of her eyebrows arched up her forehead. Her eyes narrowed as she regarded him carefully. She frowned, then reached up and unclasped the necklace, tossing it on the table. She removed her rings and earrings and added them to the pile.

"I didn't say you couldn't wear them," Lachlan said.

"If you had, I would have ignored you."

His lips quirked up again in an almost-smile. She

definitely had fire in her. It was refreshing.

"I only wore them because Hayden asked me to," Emma said. "She probably thought you made them and would want to see me wearing them."

"Why would I want that?"

"People generally like to see others using the things they gave them. She and Finn probably thought it would help us bond or something."

"I wonder what he thinks of you taking them off, then."

"Is Finn here?"

"I'd be surprised if he wasn't. He's probably lurking somewhere, observing everything."

Emma chuckled. "Hayden likes to lurk, too. They really are a matched pair."

"How does that work, anyway?" Lachlan leaned forward, eager to hear what she had to say. It could be the key to restoring the balance of power among the Fae courts who ruled over the Wheel of the Year. "This whole bonding with a specific mortal thing."

"I don't know." She shrugged and shook her head. "From all the stories, it sounds like you just look into the right person's eyes and know that something is there."

'Stories'? Did she not have any practical experience with this, either? If so, they might be in trouble. Lachlan didn't think it would be wise to draw attention to that, so he went down a different line of inquiry.

"What is the 'something?'"

Emma pursed her lips, then smiled slightly. Her eyes had a far-off look. "Magic."

"Magic?" Lachlan repeated. He didn't know what she was talking about.

"The strongest magic there is." She leaned forward, her gaze intense. "Love."

Lachlan actually laughed. He couldn't help it. Was this what Finn thought would restore the balance? Mortal daydreams and self-aggrandizement? Mortals had no magic of their own. There was no way that one of their emotions was behind the power surge in the Yuletide Fae —or Finn, for that matter.

"The strongest bullshit, maybe," Lachlan said.

Emma scowled. Somehow, watching her smile disappear unsettled him. Probably because so much was riding on them being able to work together. And love had nothing to do with that.

"I'm holding out for love," Emma said. "So you can take this fake marriage of yours and shove it up your—"

Lachlan jumped in before she could finish. "I don't give a crap what you want. Frankly, neither should you."

Her eyebrows rose and her mouth dropped open. An intriguing spark glimmered in her eye. Lachlan didn't have time to notice such trivialities, but it was hard not to see a thousand little details that made him wonder if perhaps this was a match that could work. Not through ridiculous notions like love. But perhaps together they could figure out the true root of the growth in power among the Fae and replicate it for themselves.

Emma was nothing like the obsequious members of the Fae who sought his favor in order to gain more power for themselves. No, he had a feeling she would always tell him exactly what she thought, whether it helped or hindered her position with him. If that was true, then perhaps she was someone who could be his partner in all this. She was even more outspoken than Finn.

"Wow, you really know how to sweet-talk a girl," Emma said.

"This isn't about what you want. Or what I want."

"Again with the flattering."

Lachlan continued, ignoring her sarcasm. "The balance of nature has been thrown off. The Courts of the Fae who rule over the seasons affect all the realms—both Faerie and mortal. What the Yuletide Fae started has created a domino effect and mine is the first court to feel it. I'm the first required to fix it. And if I can't… I have no idea what it will mean for your world or mine."

"Have you talked to Hayden about this? Or Finn?" Emma leaned forward aggressively, stabbing the table with her index finger. "This is entirely about what we want. I can't give you what you need, so you need to let me go."

An odd tightness grew in Lachlan's chest. She seemed to be a perfect candidate to be his queen. She was outspoken, strong, and had an unbendable will. Even without knowing how to use the power that resided within her, she was facing him down without hesitation. How could she be so eager to let go of that power and the prestige of the position?

It didn't matter. Lachlan didn't have time for this. The stakes were too high.

"Fine," he said. "If you don't want to marry me, then find someone to take your place."

"No." Emma recoiled as if the thought was anathema to her. "Absolutely not. I would never do that to another woman."

"Then you do it. Be my queen."

She let out an exasperated sigh. "You still don't get it. It wouldn't matter if I agreed to keep this title or even rule by your side. This isn't about getting married. It's about falling in love. And that's something that can't be rushed or forced or magicked into existence. Love has to grow over time. You have to nurture it."

He shook his head, letting out a sigh that matched hers. He ran his hands over his face, as if he could wipe away his obvious frustration. This was never going to work. Why had Lachlan let Finn talk him into doing this in the first place? Lachlan was stuck in a too-tight, itchy suit, in a too-quiet, too-small dining hall. There was no fresh air. No sun. Nothing to interest him.

Except Emma, who definitely wasn't interested in him.

The thought caused a strange pang to echo through his

chest, his throat tightening. Lachlan reached up and tugged at his tie, tearing it loose and tossing it on the table. The thing had been half-strangling him all night. He undid the top few buttons of his shirt, then leaned back in his chair, taking deep breaths of the stale recycled air as he tried to figure out what to do next.

When his eyes met Emma's once more, that spark was there again, except it burned differently. Her dark eyes smoldered as she stared at the skin he'd exposed. More of that strange tightness rose in his chest, much more pleasant this time. It spread down over his abdomen and to his groin. What the hell did that mean? Emma noticed him watching her intently and quickly broke off her own stare, clearing her throat.

"Look, you have a lot going for you." She waved a hand in his direction, her eyes getting that intensity again before she shook it off and very deliberately looked away. "It wouldn't be hard to find a woman who wants you. But getting her to love you? That's a different matter."

"Fine," he said. "Then teach me. Show me what it takes to get someone to fall in love with me."

Emma's lips pulled up in a smile. She shook her head and even laughed lightly. After a pause, she let out a sigh.

"I will do what I can for you," she said. "But there's a piece to this puzzle that you haven't mentioned yet. A piece that's just as important as finding the right someone and helping them to fall in love with you."

"What's that?" Lachlan asked.

"You have to fall in love with them, too."

"I can do that," he said. "If it gets me the power I need, I'll do it."

She arched that eyebrow again. An odd thrill rushed through him, sharpening his focus and suffusing his limbs with energy. Whatever was involved in this challenge, he was certain he'd be up for it. He had to admit, the idea of spending more time with Emma was appealing as well. This was the most interesting mortal he'd ever met. Possibly the most interesting person.

"You don't think I can do it," he said.

"I think it won't be as easy as you think."

"Why is that?"

She looked aside, gathering her thoughts. After a few moments, her gaze returned to him.

"Love isn't something that you just get to feel if you've never experienced it before," she said. "If you've never had love in your heart, you have to work for it. *Learn* how to feel it. And the first lesson is that love isn't about something you get, it's about something you give."

"I have to fall in love with her first?"

"It's different every time."

"I'm not interested in multiple wives."

Her eyebrows furrowed. "Good. But that's not what I'm talking about. Usually, people fall in love more than once in their lives. I guess it's different among the Fae.

Have you ever loved anyone? Your mom or dad?"

"I didn't have parents."

"How did you come into being, then?"

He opened his mouth to reply, then realized he didn't have an answer. Thinking back to his origins, he couldn't remember when or how he had started to exist. He just... was. It was unsettling to recognize the gap in his knowledge of himself, but also strangely invigorating. She was making him look at his reality from new perspectives. Now, she stared at him, patiently waiting for an answer.

"I don't have a family," he said, his voice gruff. "I have a court and I have a duty. It's my job to make sure that spring happens for all the realms. That's who I am and who I've always been."

"Okay. Let's look at your court, then. Is there anyone special in there?"

"What does that have to do with anything?"

"There are lots of different kinds of love. If we can find someone that you care about in another way, maybe we can tap into that to help you figure out how to actually fall in love with someone."

"I have to fall in love with a *mortal* to get the same boost in power as the Yuletide Court, not a member of the Fae."

Her lips tightened. She must have picked up on the frustration in his tone. How could he not be frustrated by this situation? It was all so alien to him.

"See, that's the root of your problem right there," she said. "This is just another task to you. Something to accomplish so you can reap the rewards. But love isn't about what's in it for you. It's about caring for another person more than anything. It's about passion and longing —about sleepless nights wondering what they're doing, what they're thinking, if they're happy or not and how you can help them. And wondering when they'll be in your arms again."

His brow furrowed. "That sounds terrible."

Emma laughed, her features brightening with a broad smile. He returned her smile reflexively, a strange warmth blossoming in his belly.

"It can be," she said. "Especially when you love someone and they don't feel the same way about you in return."

He sighed. "Why would anyone want this? Having such strong feelings toward someone puts you in a position of weakness."

"No, it makes you strong," she said. "When you love someone, you'd do anything for them. Things you never thought you were capable of before. Even if they don't love you back."

# Chapter Three

This was going to be a hard sell. Emma watched as Lachlan parsed through the information she was giving him, as he struggled to understand. But he was trying, and that meant something to her. He wasn't the arrogant Fae king that she'd expected. At least, she hadn't seen that side to him yet. He was driven and she suspected that there was a great deal of passion hidden in that delicious physique of his.

If they had met under different circumstances, Emma absolutely would have been interested in him. But waking from a magical trance to discover they were 'married' and she'd been sucked into the political machinations of a Fae court? Not so much.

Lachlan was staring at a spot on the table so intently, she wondered that it didn't burst into flames. She could practically hear the gears turning in his brain as he tried to figure out his next step. His hands were resting on the table, so she reached across and grasped one. He blinked, staring up at her with a guarded expression.

"Hey, it's going to be okay," she said. "We'll figure this

out."

"I wish I believed that."

When she went to pull away, he clasped her hand gently. Something in the gesture moved her. She thought she saw the slightest glimpse of vulnerability in his eyes. He glanced around at the room, then shifted in his chair, looking profoundly uncomfortable.

"Do you want to get out of here?" she asked, smiling.

"Please." He pushed back from the table and stood, towering over her. Emma almost felt as though she was standing beneath an actual oak tree.

She stood next to him, craning her neck to look up at him. "You really live up to the hype, you know that?"

"I have no idea what that means," he said, but he was smiling, too.

"What do we do with those?" She gestured toward the pile of jewelry on the table that was probably worth more than her house and everything in it.

"Leave them for Finn and Hayden. I'm sure they'll take care of it."

"Do you think they'll take care of my coat, too?"

Lachlan looked over her head at something and nodded. "It's done."

"Excellent. I want to be somewhere *else*."

Lachlan was still holding onto her hand, so she gripped it tighter and headed out of the restaurant, pulling him behind her. If they were going to do this, they were doing it her way. She didn't want Lachlan getting stuck with a woman who expected to get wined and dined at a fancy place. The last thing the world—their worlds—needed was another person only interested in power for themselves.

With Lachlan, Emma had seen a spark of something else. Potential. He was open to learning how to love someone. That went a long way in Emma's book. She wanted the person who won his heart to deserve it.

A sharp pang stabbed through her chest at the thought. She scowled, rubbing her chest lightly, willing it to go away. The feeling persisted, though. It must be some sort of side effect of them both sharing the magic of the Wheel of the Year. It absolutely was not anything like disappointment or jealousy. She looked back at him over her shoulder as they made their way through the people chatting in the restaurant's entry area. He was staying close, using his incredible bulk as interference to clear a path and keep people from bumping into her.

*Yeah. Keep telling yourself that.*

The wooden door swung open as they approached. A surprised doorman stumbled forward to grab the handle. Emma smiled at him as they passed. They hurried down the stairs, into the brisk mid-April air. Emma shivered and rubbed her arms, dropping Lachlan's hand.

"I should have thought better about ditching my coat," she said. "I just had to get out of there."

"Me, too." Lachlan took off his jacket and swung it

over her shoulders.

She glanced up at him, surprised at the thoughtful gesture. Weren't fairies supposed to be totally self-absorbed? There was even more hope for him than she'd originally thought. She was about to thank him, but stopped herself.

"I would thank you, but the stories I've read say that fairies don't like that," Emma said. "Does that apply to you?"

"It doesn't bother me one way or another. Thanking us is a way of establishing a connection. If we accept the thanks, it can create an unwanted link. If we ignore it, as I usually do, nothing happens."

"Noted. I appreciate the jacket just the same."

"For the record, I wouldn't mind if you thanked me."

His lips were pulled up in the slightest smile. Little tendrils of heat spread through her, wrapping around her bones and lighting her up. Was he saying he wanted them to be bonded? She turned and started walking down the sidewalk, kicking herself mentally. Lachlan followed.

Of course, he wanted them to be bonded. They already were. If she thanked him and he accepted it, that would be one more link. He might say he wanted to learn how to fall in love with someone and gain their love in return, but Emma was pretty sure there was part of him that still thought the entire matter would be so much easier for him if she fell for him and became his magic booster.

There was no way she was letting herself be roped into that situation. She wanted mutual passion, to be someone's everything. She definitely deserved better than to be someone's tool.

From what Hayden, Finn, Ava, and Jack had described of their own experiences, that sort of outlook wouldn't work anyway. Lachlan had to fall in love, whether he wanted to or not. The sooner Emma could convince him that he would be able to do so on his own, the sooner he would cut her loose and then she could be done with this madness. Except, Hayden and Ava would still be caught up in it.

Emma scowled as she tried to think of a way to help them, or even convince them that they needed help. Fairytales seldom ended well for the humans involved. At least, the original stories didn't. Just because Jack and Finn seemed loving and attentive now, didn't mean they would stay that way forever. Especially since they were talking about eternity.

Hayden was immortal now. Finn had inadvertently infused her with enough magic to turn her into one of the Fae. Ava had a line on some sort of immortality potion that she was planning to take when her son, Charlie, was a little older. And Emma... Emma was immortal, too. Because of what the Holly King had done, she was also part of the Fae.

A shiver passed through her that had nothing to do with

the cold.

"You know, you can use your magic to be comfortable in any clime," Lachlan said.

"Now, why would I do that when I have this nice jacket to keep me warm?"

She bumped her shoulder against his arm and smiled up at him. At first, he looked affronted, but when she sort of nodded, he relaxed and shook his head.

"Mortals, am I right?" she said.

He laughed a bit. "You certainly have a different way of interacting."

"When you have a finite lifespan, you tend to want to make the most of it."

"But you don't anymore."

"Stop," she said. They both paused on the sidewalk. Emma turned to him, unsure of what she wanted to say. What she *needed* to say. "I can't get used to this. I can't think in terms of immortality and magic. I don't want to use magic to stay warm. Because it's not mine. It's not me."

"It could be."

There was no insistence to his tone, no begging, no berating nor guilt-tripping. It was just a statement of fact. He was presenting her with an option, with data, and it really did seem as if he was willing to let her make her own decision about it.

"I guess it could," she said. "But I'm not ready to leave

behind all of the wondrous parts about being mortal."

He glanced around them, then turned his attention back to her. "Such as?"

"Such as…" Emma tilted her head back to look at the blue sky, streaks of white clouds scattered throughout her field of vision. "Those. How often do you just gaze at the sky? Do you feel a sense of wonder and awe? Or feel the distance between us and the clouds?"

He looked up and stared at the sky for a few moments, then shook his head. "I can't say that I have."

"What about puppies?"

This time, when he laughed, it was full-throated and deep. The rich sound sent all sorts of pleasant tingles running up and down her spine.

"Puppies?" he said.

"Have you ever held a puppy?"

"I can't say I've done that, either."

"Why not?"

"I've never had a reason to."

"And see, that's the difference right there. It's reason enough just to experience it. To feel its soft fur, its warm body and tiny, fast-beating heart. For us, for mortals, life is all about the living. It's about grabbing on to everything life gives you and enjoying the hell out of it. Riding the sorrows, embracing the joys. It's about holding your sides laughing with friends and holding their hands while they cry just as hard." She turned to face him. "You want me to be your queen, but what can you possibly offer me that's better than all that?"

# Chapter Four

Emma was casting a spell on him. She had to be. How could she make such a compelling argument in favor of being mortal? Why else would Lachlan's chest feel so tight, his skin prickling with awareness of how close she was? He had never had a conversation with someone that was so... grounded. He couldn't wait to hear what she would say next.

She had asked him a question. It should have been a simple one, yet he didn't have an answer. All he had was the strangest longing for more time with her.

"Instead of better, how about different?" he said.

She took a step closer. "I am intrigued."

"Can you trust me? Just a little?"

"I shouldn't. You're a fairy."

"So are you, at the moment."

She scowled at him, but when he held out his hands, she relented, moving even closer. Somehow, the closer she approached, the tighter his skin felt. When she took both his hands in hers, he pulled her closer still.

"If I didn't know better, I'd say you were making a

move on me," she said, a fascinating sparkle in her eyes.

"I'm making a move *with* you."

"What do you mean?"

He smiled, wanting to surprise her by showing her. Summoning his power, he let his magic sink deep into the earth, connecting with the energy of the leylines beneath the way a tree's roots reached for nutrients and moisture from the soil. Wind swirled up from the ground. His skin felt electrified. Green and gold light formed a spiraling column around them, spinning faster and faster. Emma shifted closer, her grip on his hands tightening. With a final flash of light, the corridor between the mortal realm and his Faerie kingdom collapsed, leaving them standing in a mushroom ring within his forest.

Emma stared at her surroundings, eyes wide and mouth hanging open. Her gaze traveled up the long stalks of mushrooms that towered over their heads, their red tops swaying high above. Lime green leaves covered the trees along with thick clumps of spring blossoms—white, pink, and purple. At their roots, bright yellow daffodils, rich purple and gold crocuses, and tulips and irises of every color made the grotto even more beautiful. It was one of Lachlan's favorite places within his kingdom.

A flock of spring pixies flew past them, their wings blurring as they performed astounding aerial maneuvers, showing off for the pair. Instead of gasping in awe, Emma started trembling. An odd tingling spread down his spine, much less pleasant than those he'd experienced previously with her. Her grip tightened further on his hands and she pressed herself against him. It would have been pleasant, if it weren't for the way she was trembling, shaking her head and staring at the pixies and the clearing around them. Lachlan summoned a gentle breeze, nudging the pixies until they flew away.

"This is Faerie," she said, a golden light sparking in her warm eyes. "You took me to Faerie."

"Not just Faerie. This is the Springtime Kingdom. Our kingdom."

"*Your* kingdom," she snapped.

Power surged out from her, flooding the ground beneath them. Veins of gold light spread across the ground as she fed energy into the leylines. Too much energy. It crawled up the trees, thickening the clumps of flowers until their branches bent under the weight of the blossoms. The gills of the mushroom caps opened, their edges curling up as the power overwhelmed them.

"This is just like the stories." She didn't look at him as she spoke, her eyes wild with fear. "I'm trapped. You'll play music and make me dance for you till my feet fall off."

"What?"

He would have laughed at the absurdity of it if she weren't so obviously afraid—an emotion he was beginning to share as her power continued to flood the land. Lachlan had suspected coming to their kingdom would heighten her power, perhaps more effectively connecting her with it. He had no idea this would happen. He had no idea how to make it stop.

"What stories have you been reading?" He tried to get her thinking, to help her regain control.

"The Brothers Grimm," she said.

"Them? They only focused on the worst of us." It shocked him how much it mattered to him already that she not see fairies as monsters—that she not see *him* that way. "Emma, please. Don't believe them."

"No. No, you'll leave me here, or... or you'll change."

She let go of one of his hands, but only so she could wrap that arm around his waist. She did the same with the other, as if they were standing at a great height and she was terrified of falling. His arms settled over her shoulders naturally and he pulled her closer. Warmth spread through him, both from her body and from within himself. He didn't understand it. He didn't understand any of this. How could he have been so wrong about sharing this with her?

"This isn't my world," she said. "This isn't my world."

It wouldn't be suitable for anyone for much longer if she kept overwhelming the leylines with her uncontrolled magic. What could he do to snap her out of this? Their realm was in major danger, her power was beyond anything he had expected. Her near-chanted words reminded him suddenly of something Finn had said when he was sharing his and Hayden's experiences.

*'When we kiss, the world falls away. It's as if the two of us are the only thing in existence, in our own world, made from our love.'*

It seemed ridiculous, but Lachlan was desperate. He didn't want to hurt Emma or worse—fuel her fear of the Fae by forcing her to stop. He wasn't even sure he could if he tried. So, instead, he clasped Emma's face in his hands and turned her toward him, then bent down to press his lips to hers.

At first she stiffened, but then her lips moved against his, soft and warm. Heat flooded him, his skin rising in gooseflesh, his heart pounding. Electric pleasure arced through every part of him as he pulled her closer. He had never felt more alive. He was hyper-aware of everywhere they touched, wanted more of it—to be closer, even though there was no space between them.

His lips opened and he thrust his tongue into her mouth. She let out a moan as she welcomed him, exploring him even as he explored her. It still wasn't enough. His hands slid to the small of her back, urging her closer. He was just about to reach down and lift her from the ground when she pushed against him.

She blinked up at him, the fear in her eyes replaced with a somewhat dazed look. Lachlan hated to admit it, but wouldn't be surprised if his had taken on a similar appearance.

"Why did you do that?" she asked.

His voice was oddly breathless when he replied. "I thought it might help you regain control of your power." He couldn't look away from her, but could sense that the energy she was feeding into the land had subsided. "Looks like I was right."

"*Right?*" She scowled, glaring at him balefully. "I did not ask for this power. I did not ask for this position. And I sure as hell didn't ask to be brought here. Now take me back."

"But—"

"You say you want me to trust you? You want me to teach you what it is to love someone? Lesson one. You listen to what they want, not what you want. And you give it to them. If what they want doesn't match up with what you want, you're not right for each other. You move on. It's that simple."

"Emma…"

"Please, Lachlan." There was a tremor to her voice that tugged at something deep in his chest. "I do not want to be here."

He stared at her for a few moments, then nodded. Calling on his power, the corridor rose around them once more, bursting with energy. He drew as much into himself as he could to stabilize their passage. Gods, how did she have so much power? This was much more than what the Holly King had bestowed on her. Were mortals able to amplify their own magic when given it as well as their Fae mates'?

Lachlan would have to think on that later. Right now, Emma needed him. Their realm needed him. She risked burning out the glade with the amount of power she was putting off.

As the golden light surrounded them, she buried her face against his chest. Lachlan had never held anyone like this or been held himself. His heart beat quickly and his chest felt tight, as if it was overfull of something. Even in the short time he'd spent with her, he had become certain that this woman was one of the strongest people he'd ever met. And he had frightened her, terribly.

A fierce protectiveness rose within him. She truly wanted nothing to do with the Fae. The thought made his breath catch. There was no way he could succeed at winning her heart or making her his queen. He would just have to take what she had offered, to learn how to win a different mortal's heart. The thought left an aftertaste of ashes. But he couldn't force her into this, especially after witnessing the extent of her power.

He pulled on more of his magic, transforming her clothing to resemble what she was wearing the first time he saw her. Jeans, a deep sapphire T-shirt, and sensible shoes. He added a Robin's egg blue sweater to keep her warm, but didn't bother to make it fancy. Instead, he opted for durability and comfort. While he was at it, he changed his own outfit to what he preferred when visiting the mortal realm—clothing similar to hers, but in muted browns accented with green.

The corridor dropped as they arrived in the center of a much smaller mushroom ring in the mortal realm. Magic leached out from them. Green blades of grass erupted at their feet, crocuses and daffodils opened, and the buds on the trees above burst into bloom. Emma kept her grip on Lachlan's waist. He was tempted to stay that way, just holding each other, but couldn't leave her in fear for a moment longer.

"We're here," he said.

"Here where?" Her voice was muffled against his chest.

"Crystal Creek park."

She pulled away slowly, blinking at the brightness of the spring sun. She still clutched the fabric of his shirt, as if she was afraid she might float away if she let go. Or maybe she was afraid she was still in Faerie and that he would leave her.

*If only she wanted me to stay near for another reason…*

She had made her feelings clear. How could she rule a realm that she was terrified to set foot in? He had never met anyone so afraid of the Fae. Lachlan had to think of his people now. Consider the balance between all the realms. And yet, his mind kept circling the memory of that kiss.

"It's quiet here," he said. "I thought it might help you get your bearings."

"Thanks." She took a cautious step forward, pulling him along with her as she eyed the circle of mushrooms that surrounded them suspiciously. "A fairy ring?"

Lachlan nodded. "At least your books got that right."

He couldn't keep the edge from his tone. Something about her reaction had affected him deeply. It wasn't just that she was rejecting the power she'd been given or the title. She was rejecting him. Everything he had to offer. He had tried to make her happy, and he had failed spectacularly.

Her lips pinched in a bloodless line, but she kept ahold of him. He followed her as she stepped out of the circle, then hurried to an asphalt trail. She stood stiffly for a few moments, taking deep breaths and letting them out slowly.

After what felt like a long time, she turned to him and in a quiet voice said, "Don't ever do that to me again."

"The kiss or the traveling?"

She glared at him, but then said, "The traveling."

"I won't. I wouldn't have done it in the first place if I'd known that was how you would react." He shook his head. "You really do hate fairies. I'd like to say I can't imagine what you think of me, but after that—"

"I don't hate fairies," Emma said, brusquely. Her voice softened as she went on. "And I don't hate you. I just… I'm scared, alright? Maybe the books I've read aren't completely accurate, but I *know* there's truth to them."

"How?"

Her mouth snapped shut again, her dark eyes blazing.

"You've encountered the Fae before," he said.

Emma looked away, shaking her head. "That's crazy."

"And that's a reflexive response. How many times have you denied whatever you experienced? Enough to start believing it never happened yourself?"

Her eyes snapped back to his. The pain and anger he saw there made him want to hit something. Strange. He'd never wanted to do that before. He grasped her free hand, hoping she wouldn't notice that she still clung to him with the other so he could enjoy that closeness for a little longer.

"There are malicious Fae," he said. "Horrible, terrifying beings."

"The Unseelie Court," she whispered.

"Yes. And the Seelie Court isn't much better. They're just nicer to look at, generally."

She snorted, her lips curving up into the tiniest smile. It seemed as if he was seeing the first crocus bloom. Lachlan shifted closer, clasping her elbow.

"We are part of the Wheel of the Year," he said. "As such, we are linked to nature herself. We belong to neither of those Courts. We're separate from them."

Her eyes narrowed. "That's not what my books said."

"The Grimm brothers corrupted the truth to suit their

own needs. Besides, they were assholes."

She actually laughed at that, but quickly shuttered her expression again. She stared at him for a long time, then said, "How do I know you're not saying all this because it's what I want to hear? You could be trying to trick me into liking you."

"Is it so hard for you to believe that you could like me just because of who I am?" His chest tightened further as the words left his lips. He couldn't believe how much her answer mattered to him. How much it mattered what she thought of him.

She stared at him in silence for a moment, then said, "Fairies aren't to be trusted."

"Yeah. A lot of us aren't trustworthy. But a lot of us are. You're putting all your faith in stories that were meant to scare children into behaving."

"Stories where fairies consistently trick humans."

"You're not human anymore. You haven't been since the Holly King placed half the magic of the Wheel of the Year inside of you."

"No."

"Emma." He shook his head fighting off exasperation. "Instead of believing what you read in a book, believe what you see with your own eyes. What you smell and hear and… And what you feel. You are the queen of the Springtime Court. That gives you more than enough power to see through any *glamour* or charm. Believe in your own perceptions. Believe in yourself. I certainly do."

# Chapter Five

This couldn't be real. Emma was staring into the eyes of the most gorgeous man she'd ever met, and he was saying all the right things to get her to drop her guard. Worse, he was making her *want* to drop her guard. The most dangerous guy she'd ever dated—*not* that they were dating—was the one getting under her skin.

*Figures.*

She sighed and shook her head. "Maybe… Maybe we have things to teach each other. But you have to wait till I'm ready instead of springing things on me like that. No pun intended."

Lachlan chuckled, but then said, "I have limited time. The next stage of the Wheel of the Year is Beltane, and that's coming up fast."

"May first, right?"

"You really do know your stuff," he said.

She smiled tensely, waiting for him to pry. He had come so close to digging out her biggest secret, but he wasn't pushing her about it, even though it might serve his purposes. Maybe he really was respecting her wishes.

Maybe he wasn't like the Fae in the stories.

Or the fairy that she had met as a child.

She shook her head quickly, hard enough to rattle the memories back into their cage. Lachlan's brow furrowed, but he still didn't ask what had prompted her to do so. She took a deep breath and let it out slowly.

"So, we have a timeline," she said. "I can work with that. But first, I really need to clear my head."

"Okay. How do we do that?"

She scowled, wondering whether she should ask him to leave. Emma had spent almost every moment with Hayden and Finn since she was given the magic of the Wheel of the Year, Finn watching over them both as they learned to deal with their new abilities. Emma was afraid the moment Lachlan left her sight, the moment she was alone, the doubts would start to rise in her mind—old doubts that had left deep scars. She didn't want to be left wondering if this had all been some kind of dream. Or worse, to be stuck telling herself over and over that fairies weren't real, so none of this could be possible. To fall back into the habit of convincing herself not to believe her own perceptions.

Lachlan had just told her to believe in herself. No one had ever said that. Not where *this* was concerned. It was exhilarating and terrifying. If she stopped turning away from the magical world that had once more opened itself up to her, would she fall into it and lose herself? Her humanity? She looked up at Lachlan, saw the earnestness in his expression, and her stomach filled with butterflies. That had never happened before.

*I felt this way when I saw him at the restaurant, before I knew he was Fae.*

More than her humanity was on the line. Her heart raced when she looked at him. Her skin prickled with awareness when he was near. And when he spoke, what he said didn't seem like a trick or a spell. For all that he was a fairy king, he seemed real in a way that no one she'd ever dated before had been. She realized in that moment that she had to see this through.

"Follow me." She released her death grip on his shirt and turned to walk down the trail. Lachlan kept her hand in his, a slight smile on his face as he glanced up at the greening trees.

After a while, she said, "Finn is doing a good job helping spring along."

"He is. I worried about him at first, when I gave him the job. He didn't seem the right fit, but he's exceeded my expectations at every turn."

"Why did you think he couldn't do it?"

"Have you seen how he dresses?" Lachlan laughed. "I didn't think he'd really get what it means to help spring along. But he has his own way of getting his job done. He's more focused on the aesthetics. The flowers and colors are always more vibrant when he's on the job."

'Vibrant,' not 'impressive.' Emma had to admit, she

liked the way Lachlan thought. And it didn't match what she'd read in most of her fairytale books. Fairies were supposed to be completely self-centered and self-serving. At least Lachlan seemed to value things beyond power and influence.

They had reached the edge of town and strolled along the sidewalk in front of a row of houses. Most had flowerbeds, flower boxes, or a mix of the two in their yards. Even this early in the year, they were filled with spectacular colors. Tulips and irises in every shade, daffodils shining like little yellow suns that cheerfully swayed in the slight breeze, and beautiful clusters of crocuses.

If she was going to get sucked into the affairs of the Fae, at least it was for her favorite season. Not that she was okay with it or giving in at all. She was just gathering information. Figuring out more about her 'co-ruler.'

"I'm curious—what does helping spring along mean to you?" she asked.

"It's about helping the seeds to sprout and grow deep roots so they can handle the monumental growth of summer." He lifted his free hand in front of him, gazing at it as if imagining soil marking his palm. "Spring is about getting your hands dirty. About digging into the earth and feeling her energy. Feeding and supporting it and following the cycles of nature."

"You don't just use magic all the time?"

"No." He shook his head, a distant look in his eyes and a soft smile on his face. "There are some things you just have to experience. Besides, getting your hands in the soil has its own magic."

Emma stared up at him, one eyebrow quirked. "So… you're a king who works the land?" That was hard to believe even of a mortal king.

"What?" he said. "Just because I'm a fairy, I can't know how to farm?"

She laughed and shook her head. "I guess it makes sense. It still surprises me, though."

"You thought fairies wear fancy suits and dresses all the time?"

An image flashed into her mind of a small gray cat with a tuft of white at her throat, her legs tucked underneath her body and her tail flicking lazily as she slept in the sun. Emma shuddered, pulling her hand free from Lachlan's so she could hug her middle. She scowled and shook her head.

"No, I don't," she said. Before he could say anything, she nodded toward the house they were approaching. "We're here."

"Where's here?"

"Home."

She opened the gate on her white picket fence and gestured for him to go first. He quickly scrutinized everything as he walked inside. The house was powder blue with white trim and pale yellow shutters. Blueberry bushes clustered around her front porch with myriad flowering bulbs beneath them. The cobblestone walkway that led to the house was flanked by four raised beds that took up most of the yard, with river rock and flagstones between them. The first sprouts of the Swiss chard, kale, and lettuce she'd recently seeded were pushing through the soil and she could see the tips of her asparagus starting to come back.

Lachlan paused, his lips slightly parted as he stared at her front garden. "This is…"

"Tiny?" She frowned, imagining how it must look compared to the wonders of his Springtime kingdom. "Mundane?"

"Wonderful," he broke in before she could say more. "This is wonderful."

"Why?" She crossed her arms over her chest. "Because it makes us more compatible?"

He chuckled. "I guess it does. But no, it's just… wonderful. May I?" He squatted down, one hand poised above the soil.

Emma stepped forward her hands suddenly at her sides, ready to… do something. Knock him over, if she had to.

"No magic," she said. "Giving or taking."

His eyebrows drew closer as he scowled back at her. "It's not always about giving or taking. Sometimes—the best times—it's just about *being*."

She felt her mouth drop open, but couldn't think of a single thing to say. Instead, she watched as he gingerly burrowed his hands into the soil, turning his full attention to what he was doing, what he was experiencing. His brow smoothed, that slight smile she'd seen so often on his face returning. She liked that smile. And she loved that all it took to bring it out was a moment—this moment—with her garden.

He lifted some of the dirt and crumbled it between his fingers, his smile deepening. "This is excellent soil. It must have taken scores of years to get it like this." He glanced up at her, an unspoken question in his eyes.

"My grandparents." Suddenly, her throat felt tight, her eyes filled with moisture. She coughed lightly, turning away. "It's my grandparents' house. They gave it to me when they moved into an assisted living facility." Emma visited as often as she could and constantly sent them pictures of the gardens and the cherished home she'd been entrusted with.

Lachlan rose, dusting off his hands. His smile turned into a gentle smirk.

"What?" she said, a bit of an edge to her voice.

"I was just thinking of something Finn said to me recently. 'Mortals can't rely on magic, so they instead turn to each other. They work together to achieve their common goals.'"

"Well, yeah." She gestured to the gardens. "We get the

job done, even if it's not as flashy or quick as—"

"It's wonderful." He reached out and clasped her hands in his.

She narrowed her eyes at him. "You're just saying that to try to make me like you."

"I'm saying it because it's true." He tugged on her hands. A shiver of excitement raced up her spine as he pulled her closer. "But if I were just saying it to get you to like me... would it work?"

# Chapter Six

Lachlan's breath stilled as he watched Emma, waiting for her reaction, hoping he hadn't overstepped. Her beautiful lips pulled into a soft frown, but then almost immediately curled back up into a smile. She turned toward the house, but kept one of her hands in his, pulling him along behind her.

"Let's go," she said.

He followed willingly, almost happily. The emotion surprised him as much as her gardens had. She might say she wasn't interested in being his partner, but the more time they spent together, the more certain he grew that she was exactly the woman he needed—that he *wanted*—at his side. Her yard was like her own sacred grove, and she had to spend quite a bit of time on it for it to be so well-kept. More than that, the energy that he could sense in the soil, the warmth and care, convinced him that she would be the perfect Springtime Queen.

The Fates were at work here. Lachlan knew better than to go against them. All he had to do was convince Emma that they belonged together.

She led him up a short set of steps to her porch. A white swing hung from the ceiling, suspended by lengths of chain. The breeze flowed past them, carrying a slight tinge of iron. He fought the urge to sneeze. She opened the door, looking back to address him over her shoulder.

"I somehow doubted that Finn and Hayden remembered to lock up when they took me to our date," she said. "Which is a good thing, because I totally forgot to bring along my purse."

He followed her into a cozy living room. Bright sunlight streamed in from half a dozen windows. Gauzy curtains hung over them to provide privacy while letting in the light, with a sturdier fabric in deep magenta on their sides. The floors were hardwood, worn with age, but well-kept. A small navy blue couch and two goldenrod cushioned chairs sat at the edges of a rug in matching colors, surrounding a small coffee table covered in cookbooks. She pushed the door shut behind them, then kept moving through a small hallway that led to a kitchen. Lachlan had to duck to keep from hitting his head on the lintel.

If the living room had appeared cozy, the kitchen was a welcoming harbor. A rich mahogany island stood in the center of the space. Above it, a rack hung from the ceiling, supporting a dozen pots and pans in copper, blue, and shining steel. Half of the wall to their left was taken up with an enormous refrigerator. The rest held a dishwasher, a microwave set above a double oven, and a large stove with a huge hood leading to an impressive vent that fed into the wall and presumably vented outside. The center of the wall contained a picture window above a large sink.

An archway to his right led into a dining room. The rest of the right wall was covered in cabinets in the same dark mahogany as the kitchen island, along with shelves filled with spices and more cookbooks. Lachlan's gaze was drawn to the windows opposite them, though. They flanked a door that led to the back yard. The windows were huge, their curtains drawn back to reveal a view of more raised beds and fruit trees covered in blossoms.

"No wonder my favorite grove didn't impress you," Lachlan said. "You live in a paradise of your own."

"I never said it didn't impress me." She released her grip on him and hurried to the sink. Once she was there, she started vigorously washing her hands. "I just didn't want to be there."

He could tell there was a story behind her words, behind her fear. Something that involved the Fae. He also sensed that pushing her on the topic would only drive her further away. She was as skittish as a deer who had narrowly escaped a hunter. Lachlan's hands curled into fists at the thought. Who had frightened her so badly?

*How can I make them pay?*

The thought surprised him. He had never felt vengeful before on another's behalf. The emotion rose up in him, flooding him with an unfamiliar energy. He shook it off, trying to keep his attention on Emma and the present moment.

"Wash up," she said, moving to the fridge.

He did as instructed, mimicking what he'd seen her do. Iron didn't bother Fae of the Wheel of the Year as much as the other courts, but his skin was still itching when he finished. It was strange that Emma didn't seem bothered at all. Perhaps becoming Fae herself hadn't changed her as much as he might have thought.

"If you don't know your way around a kitchen, you're about to learn," she said.

"I don't have experience, but I studied cooking and kitchens over the past two weeks."

She glanced over at him, her surprise obvious. "Why would you do that?"

"Why do you think?"

He let the question hang between them. Instead of answering, her lips tightened into a line. She turned back to the fridge and started pulling out ingredients and handing them to him.

"Put this all on the island," she said.

"Mind telling me what we're doing?"

"We're stress baking. Specifically, we're making a chocolate cake."

Given what he knew of her, it made sense. He carried the items she handed him to the kitchen island, then watched as she gathered bowls, two circular pans, and an assortment of measuring cups and spoons. She settled into a focused routine, bringing the ingredients together while instructing him as they went along. There was a cool detachment in her interactions, as if she'd done this a thousand times and he was like every other person she'd taught. The thought conjured a dull ache in his chest.

If this was what she needed to normalize, he'd go along with it. He just hoped at some point she would actually look at him, talk to him, let him know what was going on in her head. He'd never been so intrigued by anyone before. She didn't seem to share his interest, though. The moment the cakes were in the oven, she started on the icing. This time, she worked in reverse, pointing out ingredients and tools she was done with and telling him where to put them away.

She was finishing with loading the dishwasher when the oven beeped to let them know the cakes were done. Lachlan was standing nearby and he opened the door to remove the pans. Heat warmed his face as the hot air contained inside blasted outwards. The most amazing scent came with it, rich and chocolaty.

As he reached inside, Emma began to yell, "Hot mitts! Hot mitts!"

He paused, then straightened, turning to face her. It was the first sign of emotion he'd seen from her since they started 'stress baking.'

"If that's a nickname for me, I'm not sure I like it," he said.

She let out a brief laugh, then forced a scowl. "I was trying to keep you from burning yourself."

She pulled on a pair of oversized oven mitts that had been hanging next to the oven, then reached in and pulled out the pans one after another. A set of cooling racks were waiting nearby, so she set them there, then closed the oven door, turned it off, and hung the 'mitts' back up again.

"I appreciate the sentiment," Lachlan said. "But it wouldn't have hurt me."

"Really?" She shook her head. "Guess it's good to be a fairy king."

"And a queen."

Her scowl deepened. "How is it that we have time to do all this? Don't you have obligations?"

"Of course. But spending this time together is more important."

"More important than your kingly duties?"

He laughed. "I would count this among them. Besides, I have Finn to handle the minutia."

"It's not right to use people so you can do what you want."

"I'm not using him." An unpleasant tightness rose in Lachlan's chest. "I'm matching his skills and interests with the tasks that need to be completed. Finn loves that stuff. Have you seen how meticulously he dresses? I don't make him do that."

"I guess you have a point there."

"Don't you ever ask Hayden for help with things she's better at than you?"

Emma pulled a face half-way between a smirk and a frown. After a moment, she nodded.

"I guess so," she said. "Hayden sometimes gives me color palettes for my baking. She's better at that kind of stuff than I am. Her ideas and plans are amazing, but her implementation isn't always that great. She's straight-up terrible in the kitchen. I have a stool for her where she can keep me company and observe, and still be out of harm's way." She nodded toward a mahogany stool resting near one of the big windows. "I guess I'll have to get another one so Finn can join her."

"Or maybe a bench seat. Those two really seem to enjoy their proximity."

Emma's cheeks darkened. "You seemed to enjoy our proximity earlier."

"That was actually advice from Finn."

She turned to him, one eyebrow arched.

"Finn told me that when he and Hayden are… close… it seems as if the world falls away around them," Lachlan said. "You were distressed by the world we were in, so I thought it might help."

Her scowl returned, sharper than ever. "So you kissed me to manipulate me."

"No, I did it to help you. Your powers were out of control."

"I'm not really seeing a difference."

Was she absolutely determined to only see the worst in him? His heart ached at the thought.

"It worked, didn't it?" He said. When she kept scowling at him, he shrugged and went on, hoping that by opening up to her she might find a way to start to trust him, to know that he was different than all the stories she'd read. "It sure worked for me. I've never felt anything like it."

"You've never kissed anyone before?"

He shook his head. "Not like that. The Springtime Kingdom was in danger. My job—my entire purpose in existing—is to protect it. But in that moment, the only thing I could think about was you. I was invigorated. My heart was racing, my skin prickling with energy."

"Lust," she said. "Your body was flooded with desire. It happens."

"But at the same time, I felt a sense of balance and peace, of rightness, that I'd never experienced before. How can someone be flooded with desire and absolutely content at the same time?"

Her lips pulled into a thin line. She seemed to be struggling with the urge to speak. Finally, she said, "Humans don't have an eternity to accumulate experiences. We sometimes feel everything all at once."

That made sense with their brief lifespans. The idea of Emma going back to that, of her existence becoming so finite, intensified the ache in his chest. He couldn't stand the thought of losing the chance to kiss her, to explore more of these feelings.

"For the Fae, our emotions are singular and enduring," he said. "That's probably why we don't feel most things as deeply as humans. When we do, we can have rages that last for decades, sorrow that cripples us for centuries."

"That sounds awful," she said.

"It's how we are. At least, it's how I thought we were. Before today. It reminded me of something Hayden said."

"Hayden?"

"She and Finn have both lent their insight to our unique situation."

"I bet they have," Emma said, with a wry grin.

"Hayden said that the emotion of love can sometimes be created by acts of love. That if I want to experience the feeling of love within myself, the best way to do so is through acts of love toward others. I'm assuming that includes both caring actions and things like our kiss."

Emma's smile gentled. "That sounds like Hayden. But you should know that's not a guarantee that the person will ever love you in return."

"I'd still like to feel it again," Lachlan said.

"What exactly?"

"All of it."

# Chapter Seven

The idea of helping Lachlan learn about the ins and outs of relationships was more appealing than Emma wanted to admit. She just had to be careful that she didn't let down her guard and develop actual feelings for him. The way they had fallen into step, working side-by-side in the kitchen as if they'd been partners there forever... It would be so easy to do.

He didn't act like any of the fairies in the stories she had read. And he certainly didn't act like her ideas about kings. In fact, Lachlan was one of the most down-to-earth people she'd ever met. He didn't mind getting messy. He didn't mind being told what to do. He was open to her feedback—eager to receive it even. And she had the strongest feeling that it wasn't because he was trying to manipulate her.

What if all the stories she'd read were wrong?

No, not *all* of them. She had seen the frightening side of the Fae. Her left wrist still ached during bad storms sometimes. Now that she had seen fairies as an adult, she could view her childhood memories in a new light. Not as the fanciful imaginings of a bored little girl, but the actual experiences she'd had. The magic and the terror. It had all been real.

The last time she'd become friends with a fairy, her heart had been broken. Looking up at Lachlan, at his earnest expression and gorgeous… everything… He was so much more dangerous. Not to her physically. She somehow trusted that he would never hurt her. But it would be all too easy to fall for him.

No emotional involvement. She could do that. Keeping her distance was her superpower. She never let guys into her heart. But from time to time, she did let them into her bed. Lachlan had asked Emma to teach him how to fall in love. From what Hayden had shared with Emma, sex was definitely part of that for the Fae.

"You want me to help you feel everything," Emma said.

"As much as you can."

She leaned on the kitchen island, one hand resting on her hip. "That's a pretty tall order."

Lachlan took a step closer. "I'm sure you're up to the task."

She stared at him for a few moments, her thoughts buzzing. This could go wrong so many ways. But it could also go right…

"I guess that is part of what you need to know," she began, "but let's get one thing straight. I am not going to fall in love with you."

"I'm not asking you to."

She couldn't keep herself from smirking at that. He was just the right amount of cocky, tempered with his willingness to listen and remain open-minded. It was a heady mix.

"So, you shouldn't fall in love with me, either," she said.

"Duly noted." His lips pulled into a smirk that matched hers. "Is there a reason you're giving me this dire warning right now?"

She reached out and ran her fingertips along his corded forearm. Even though he held himself completely still, she could feel a tightly harnessed energy emanating from him. She stepped closer and grasped his hand in hers, then looked up at him.

"Close your eyes," she said. He hesitated for a moment, then sighed and did as she instructed. "Imagine that this moment—this very moment—is all you will ever have, so you need to experience absolutely everything. Listen to the wind in the trees. Really hear it, rustling through their leaves. Take a deep breath and smell the flowers right outside the window."

She studied his face as his lips twisted in a wry smile. As king of the Springtime Court, flowers were probably something he was well acquainted with. But as someone who lived with a bunch of fairies who used magic for everything, she was certain she could come up with many new experiences for him.

"Savor the scent of the freshly baked cake that's lingering in the air," she said.

One eyebrow arched, though he kept his eyes shut. He took another deep breath, then another, through parted lips. He smiled, then laughed.

"It's like an echo," he said. "It both is and isn't there."

"The anticipation is half the fun in baking," she said. "And other things."

She reached up and ran her fingertips over his cheek, brushing her thumb across his lips. He sucked in a breath, his eyes flying open and flashing with a bright green light. Her heart pounded, her skin tingling with anticipation. Tightening her grip on his hand, she turned and led him from her kitchen toward the curving staircase that led to the second floor. He didn't say anything, even when she pushed the door to her bedroom open and walked inside. They stopped at the foot of her bed, staring into each other's eyes.

It should have been corny. Any other time, with any other person, it would have been corny. But they had an understanding, she and Lachlan. They would explore this for their own mutual benefit, then go their separate ways. A pang echoed through her chest at the thought. It was no doubt a product of them being linked through the magic of the Wheel of the Year. She pushed the thought away and brought her hands up to the back of his neck, pulling him down for a kiss.

Just before their lips touched, he murmured, "I have a feeling I'm going to enjoy your tutelage."

She chuckled, then said, "Not half as much as I am."

His lips caught hers, commanding and fierce. There was no soft exploring, only a desperate hunger that fed into her own. He gripped the small of her back, pressing her closer, arching over to bring more of their bodies together. He was so tall. She could definitely see why they called him 'The Oak King.'

She pressed on his shoulders attempting to get him to sit down, but he didn't budge, not even when she kept up the pressure. That could get annoying fast. He didn't seem interested in breaking off the kiss, either. Physical queues seemed lost on him. She'd need to be a bit more aggressive.

Energy coiled within her, then stretched through her like a searchlight blazing toward the sky. She pushed again, and he went right down, landing heavily on the bed. He stared up at her with wide eyes.

Shit. Had she drawn on her magic? No, not *her* magic. The *fairy* magic inside of her. She didn't want to use it, didn't want to be tempted to keep it. That was one of the ways fairies tricked people, by giving them power and corrupting them with it.

But Lachlan hadn't been the one to give her the power.

The Holly King had done so. Lachlan seemed mad about it, but he wasn't taking that anger out on her. He didn't blame her unjustly, as was done in so many of the stories. From everything she'd seen of him or had learned through Finn and Hayden, Lachlan had only been decent.

Warmth bloomed in her chest at the thought. The thought she should not be having, least of all now. She needed to push it out of her head. She wanted all the worlds to go away and just give her this moment. This moment... with him.

She pulled her shirt over her head and tossed it aside, grateful she'd already removed her sweater while they were working in the kitchen. Grasping Lachlan's face, she pulled him close for another kiss. This time, she was the conqueror. She licked the seam of his lips, then plunged her tongue within as soon as he opened his mouth for her. Immediately, they were sparring, their tongues dancing, exploring, dominating. Nothing about him was passive. She loved that.

*Appreciated* that. Appreciated.

She needed more of them touching. More distraction. Pushing back from him, she bent down to untie her shoelaces.

Lachlan let out a groan and said, "Please let me use magic for that."

"Don't bother begging." Emma smiled up at him, pulling off her boots. "This is all part of the process."

She stood and shimmied out of her jeans, then kicked them aside, her socks quickly following, along with her panties and bra. Lachlan's lips were clenched in a thin line. A muscle in his jaw twitched as his gaze roved over her body. The air around him vibrated with a low growl emanating from deep in his chest. Finally, he blew out a breath, then grabbed his shirt and tore it off as he rose to his feet.

Emma felt her jaw drop, her eyes widening at the sight of his bare chest. It wasn't just the rows of perfect abs, the muscles upon muscles upon muscles. His chest and arms were covered with the most beautiful tattoo she'd ever seen. Lines wove together to form the image of bark on his chest and stomach, curving into branches that flowed down his arms. The leaves were so lifelike, they seemed to move in an unfelt breeze.

She reached out with shaky fingers, tracing the patterns. She had half expected his skin to be as rough as the tree patterned on his body, but it was warm and smooth to her touch. He hissed in a breath as her fingertips roved over his chest. She looked up to see his eyes glowing with an intense green light. He might not be using his magic, but he *was* magic. She needed to remember that. She was playing with fire here, but in that moment, she didn't care if she was burned. There was no doubt in her mind that they were about to consume each other.

Kneeling, she untied his boots and held them as he

stepped out of them. She helped him out of his socks, then rose on her knees and undid the clasp of his jeans. She pulled them down, along with his boxers, keeping her eyes averted until they were off and she had flung them away. This was something she wanted to take her time with, blocking out her peripheral view as much as she could.

She let her scrutiny slowly travel up his legs, tracing more patterns, but these lines thinner, entwined like roots. The design was beautiful, but not as beautiful as the form beneath them. His legs were as thick with muscle as the rest of him, absolutely sculpted. She couldn't resist letting her hands join her eyes in enjoying him. Reaching out, she ran her fingers along his thighs, finally letting herself look at the enormous erection jutting at her.

"Oh damn." Pleasure crashed along her nerves, her core pulsing at just the sight of him. "That is going to be a challenge."

"What do you mean?" His voice was raspy, deep with desire.

"I mean we need to make sure I'm ready before anything happens."

His brow furrowed as if he was confused. Did fairies use magic to warm up before sex? She pushed the thought of fairy foreplay out of her head, focusing on the moment.

"You might be ready to go, but my body needs… How do I say this… It needs to be prepared to receive you," she said, running the backs of her fingertips along the inside of his thighs.

He sucked in another quick breath. She loved that she could make him feel this. A powerful Fae king. She wanted to bring him more pleasure, to give him an experience he'd never forget. Even when he was with whatever human woman he eventually won. And after seeing him like this, she was sure he could have his pick of any woman he wanted. Attracting them would be easy, making them fall for him even easier. His strength was tempered with a surprising supportiveness. If he wasn't Fae, he'd be the perfect man.

*Does it really matter that much?*

Emma shoved the thought away. She wasn't going to fall for him. That was their deal. She wanted to be free. Didn't she?

She didn't want to think. She just wanted to feel. And Lachlan was eager to help with that. If this time with him was all she was going to get, she wanted to make the most of it.

"Tell me what you need, and I'll do it," Lachlan said, his voice tight.

"Stimulation." She looked up at him and smirked. "And simulation."

# Chapter Eight

Emma was staring up at him, green flickers of light sparkling in her dark eyes. Lachlan had no idea what she was thinking or planning to do. Strangely, the thought didn't unnerve him as it usually would. Emma was honest, open, and direct. There wasn't a hint of subterfuge around her. He might actually trust this woman.

His times with other Fae couldn't be called intimate. They were all transactional. Sealing agreements or creating temporary magic bindings to power spells. This feeling of anticipation she had described had a magic all its own.

She smirked as if she could hear his thoughts. He reached out and dusted his fingertips across her cheek. Her smile faltered for a moment, then she broke eye contact, staring at his dick. His chest tightened with an unpleasant feeling. He'd never been subjected to such scrutiny. What was running through that sharp mind of hers?

He was about to ask when she ran her hands up over his thighs, then leaned forward and brushed her cheek along his shaft. His nerves lit up like the bonfires of

Beltane, heat flooding through his body. What was she doing? Whatever it was, he wanted more.

She reached up and gripped his shaft, giving it a long, firm stroke. Lachlan let out a guttural sound unlike anything he'd heard from himself in all his existence. More pleasure cascaded through him, his muscles tightening, his fingers curling with the urge to grab her. But if he did, then this exquisite torture would be over.

Once more, she smirked at him as if she could read his mind. He found himself smiling back, even though in this power play, he was at an extreme disadvantage. He needed to observe, to learn, to figure out how to bring the same pleasure to her. Ideas were just beginning to form when she brought her lips to his crown, opening her mouth and running her tongue along its ridge.

All thoughts vanished as the most intense pleasure he'd ever felt crashed through his body. He hadn't known his nerves could experience bliss, but beneath her hands, in her mouth, he was finding a kind of ecstasy he hadn't realized existed. She brought her other hand to his shaft, both squeezing him tight as she continued to rhythmically stroke him. While she did, she worked as much of him into her mouth as she could, swirling her tongue over his most sensitive skin.

Pressure built within him, a pounding pulse warning him that she was too adept with her attentions. He wanted to be inside her, wanted her writhing beneath him. He grabbed her shoulders, urging her away. She glanced up at him, her eyebrows furrowed. Something she saw in his face must have explained his actions, because she rose to stand close to him. She wrapped her arms around his neck and pulled him down for a deep, passionate kiss.

He lifted her from her feet and spun them toward the bed. She clasped her legs around his waist, enabling him to crawl up the bed without breaking their kiss. He pressed her against the soft mattress and wanted nothing more than to plunge into her, but she had warned him that he needed to make her body ready. 'Stimulation and simulation.' She had certainly done that for him. Now, it was his turn.

He kissed a trail down her neck and along her collarbones, lingering when she shivered or hissed in a breath. Every time, an answering pleasure echoed through him. His dick throbbed with the need to fill her. He palmed one of her small breasts, running his thumb across her nipple. She gasped, her body arching against him. He caught her other tight nub between his lips, flicking it with his tongue. Emma burrowed her fingers through his hair, her nails running across his scalp and sending waves of electric sensation through him. Goosebumps cantered over his skin. His chest was so full, he could barely breathe.

While he continued his attentions to her breasts, he brushed his hand down to the soft curls at the apex of her legs. She moaned as he slid his fingers through her slit, gathering her wetness. Circling her clitoris with his thumb, he slid two fingers deep within her core, stretching his fingers as he thrust them in and drew them out rhythmically. She let out a plaintive noise, tugging on his hair.

"Lachlan…"

A thrum of power shuddered through him as she spoke his name. Not the magic he was used to, but something new. Something different. It wasn't even his truename, yet he felt the pull of it in his soul.

He pulled his hand away, lifting himself above her so that his crown barely parted her wet flesh. She wrapped her legs around his waist, urging him forward. He wanted to wait, to go slowly, but the temptation she presented was too great. He thrust himself deep, her channel parting for him, squeezing him tight. Nothing had ever felt so good.

She let out a cry, her nails digging into his back. Before he could ask if she was alright, she said, "More."

Lachlan rocked his hips against hers, loving how she rose to meet each thrust. Her core pulled against him, as if her body didn't want to let him part from her. The friction was driving him nearly insane with a need for more. Emma dragged her fingernails along his back, the added sensation taking him higher. She gripped his ass, urging him to land harder each time he thrust back into her.

Heat pooled within him, coalescing where they were joined. He felt it reflected from her body, as her sex began to pulse around him. She arched beneath him, crying out as her climax tore through her. Each wave of pleasure conjured an answering bliss deep within him. It coiled tight, then burst forth in an explosion of ecstasy unlike anything he'd ever known. He lost himself in the sensations, the energy coursing through him obliterating all thought. When he came back to his senses, Emma lay beneath him, a soft smile on her face as her chest heaved with quick breaths.

"Well, that did not disappoint," she said.

He smiled, then leaned down and kissed the nape of her neck. "I'm glad to hear it. Because I found it absolutely extraordinary."

The slightest tremor fluttered beneath his touch. He pulled back to look at her, but she wouldn't meet his eyes. Her lips were pressed together in a thin line and her eyes glittered oddly.

"We should probably finish up that cake," she said, her voice a bit raspy.

Lachlan stared at her for a moment, then rolled to the side. She slid out from beneath him and shimmied to the edge of the bed. He stayed where he was, watching as she dressed. How could she move on from something that had been so special? Had she not found it so? A pang skittered through his chest at the thought.

When she was dressed, she turned toward him and said, "Are you coming?"

"Yeah."

He rose from the bed, warming a bit at the way her cheeks flushed and her eyes smoldered as she looked at him. She definitely desired him physically. But he suddenly realized that he wanted more. He wanted a true partner. Someone to help him guide his kingdom and everyone within. Listening to her, learning about her, he was certain she would be the perfect person to take on that role. He *wanted* it to be her. But the way she was acting, she still seemed to want nothing to do with it.

Not bothering to hide his magic, he summoned a swirling vortex of energy that wrapped around him, conjuring an outfit similar to the one he'd worn before. Emma's lips tightened and she looked away. How could he win her heart when she was so set against the magic he possessed? And what had happened to make her turn away from it so vehemently?

He could only hope that she would share her past with him. And maybe, somehow, they could find a way toward a future together.

# Chapter Nine

Being back in the kitchen wasn't the cure-all Emma had hoped it would be. Usually, just entering this space that was so sacred to her would ease her soul and make her feel protected. It couldn't overcome the war going on in her heart. She was actually more soothed by the man standing beside her, helping her to ice their cake with barely any need for words. Shivers flooded her body every time his arm brushed against hers or his fingers grazed her hand when he gave her something she requested. He wasn't pushing her to talk or do anything. He seemed utterly content just to be with her.

There was no getting around it. Lachlan was amazing.

Without his magic, he was the most appealing man she'd ever encountered. With his magic… Well, that wasn't something she could let herself think about. How could anyone resist the idea of an insanely gorgeous, passionate—yet reserved—magical fairy king come to sweep her off her feet? Emma couldn't let herself think of him that way. It was too tempting, even with what she knew of the Fae.

She was still drawn to him, and it wasn't just physical attraction, either. If that was the only thing going on, she'd be absolutely fine. He was obviously intelligent. He was reasonable and down-to-earth in a way that she found irresistible. From what he said, he actually cared about his people and his realm, which was something she didn't think the Fae were capable of. But that was the problem. She still wasn't sure she could trust anything he said or even did. It could all be a trick to convince her to remain the Queen of the Springtime Fae.

How was this serving him? Fairies were self-serving beings. It was just in their makeup. One moment, they would be loving, beautiful, and familiar. The next, they could transform into a raging beast with sharp claws and fangs. She shuddered as long buried memories bubbled to the surface of her mind.

She didn't need the Grimm brothers to tell her fairies were dangerous. She knew it, first-hand. The Fae became something unrecognizable when they felt slighted or wronged. And those were the ones who were obvious about it. The ones who hid their ire were so much more dangerous.

What would happen if she offended Lachlan someday? How would he change and what would it do to her heart if she decided to give it to him?

*If I haven't already…*

"I used to spend my summers here, with my

grandparents." Emma was startled to hear herself speak. Her voice sounded strange and distant, even to herself, as the words poured out of her. Was she really going to share this with him?

Her heartbeat quickened, but she felt oddly calm, as if she was detached from what she was about to say. She finished the last bit of icing and stared down at the cake. Lachlan handed her a plate without saying anything. Somehow, his practical silence bolstered her.

"It was magic," she said, cutting them each a big slice and setting it on the plates he provided. "Like, the best kind of generic, non-fairy childhood magic you could experience."

She headed to the fridge to get the milk and poured them each a glass. When they were settled at the island once more, each sitting on their own stool with everything put away, she paused, wanting to see Lachlan's reaction to both the cake and what she had to say. She nodded toward the plate to encourage him to try it. He took a bite and his eyes widened for a moment before rolling closed. He shook his head, then took another.

"This is the best thing I've ever tasted," he said.

"I don't believe that. There are tons of stories about the food in Faerie luring mortals to their demise."

He nodded, still shoveling cake into his mouth, then took a big drink. Emma was mesmerized, watching the tendons and muscles flex as he tilted his head back. Even his neck was sexy. She turned her attention to her own piece and took a bite.

"Okay, this isn't half bad," she murmured.

"I've heard people complain of chemical tastes in processed food."

Emma blinked up at him, surprised that he had heard of that. It was a mundane fact for him to know about humans.

"Fae food is like that to me," he said. "It's all conjured. None of it is real."

She arched an eyebrow and smirked. "So, you don't like it because you can taste the magic in it?"

He smiled back, nodding again. "Exactly. But this cake has better magic about it."

Her heart clenched, alarm shooting through her. "You didn't cast a spell on it while we were baking, did you?"

"Of course not." He leaned over the island and smiled at her. "Its only magic is that we created it together."

She grimaced, hoping it would cover up the butterflies swarming in her stomach. "Smooth," she said.

"Truth. And you were about to share yours."

Her grimace became more authentic as she settled back on her stool. She still wanted to tell him this. He had shown her nothing but kindness. He deserved to know. She *wanted* him to know, to understand why they could never be together.

*Or maybe help me work my brain around this block so we can.*

No. No, that was not what she wanted. She just needed him to understand so he would help her get rid of this power and go back to her simple mortal life. Without him.

Her appetite fled at the thought. She pushed her plate away and forced herself to continue her tale.

"This house is in one of the oldest parts of town," she said. "You didn't get to see much on our walk back from the park, but the neighborhood only gets cooler the farther into town you get from the forest. There are tons of little shops not far away. I would be out every day exploring the neighborhoods. The houses were so cool, it was just insane."

The more she spoke, the easier it became to find the words. She could see the big Victorians with their gingerbread embellishments lining the streets toward the edge of town, remembered walking along cobblestone paths in the more 'downtown' area, with narrow buildings clustered together, each with its own distinct architecture and personality.

"When I was seven, I found this small alley or alcove I'd never noticed before." She leaned closer, resting her arm on the island's countertop. "It was barely wider than a doorway. I just had to see what was there. I came across this immaculate little garden filled with herbs. One of the walls was brick, with a lion's head fountain built into it, water trickling down for the plants in circular channels surrounded by stone walkways that made up their beds. It was incredible. I never saw another person there, just this charcoal gray cat."

She felt herself smile even as moisture rose in her eyes and her hands began to tremble. "She loved to lounge in the sun. Every day, I'd find her on this stone bench, curled up and just watching me. Until, gradually, she'd be sitting, then standing, then running to greet me."

Her heart filled with warmth at the happy memories of petting her soft fur, still warm from the sun. They would sit on the bench together while Emma read for hours. The cat seemed to like hearing Emma's voice and would paw at her books if she wasn't reading them aloud.

"It was my secret place," Emma said. "Just me and that cat. I brought her snacks every day. I've been a compulsive-feeder for as long as I can remember. That's what started me off on being really interested in the kitchen. I would bake her different cookies. God, she loved cookies. That probably should have been my first clue that she wasn't like other cats…"

A shudder flowed through her, the familiar fear rising within her as well as the shame others put on her for 'making up stories.' Emma pushed it all aside. She had to get through this.

Reassuring warmth surrounded her, flowing up from the earth and sealing her in what felt like a loving embrace. Green light tinged her periphery. Lachlan's magic. She knew the feel of it now, but it didn't worry her this time. It encircled her, but she felt something pushing back against it. The magic that had been placed within her. He was probably protecting her kitchen, protecting this part of the mortal realm to make sure she didn't damage anything if she lost control again.

He was probably protecting her.

That knowledge gave her the courage to go on.

"I didn't know her name, so I called her Junebug." She laughed and shook her head, her smile growing, even as tears welled in her eyes. Emma couldn't believe she could laugh during this, but Lachlan being close was making her feel safer somehow. She couldn't believe it, but there it was. "She would sit in my lap and purr and purr while I read to her."

Emma looked down, tugging at the napkin she held in her hands. She didn't even remember picking it up. Her smile was gone now, a cold foreboding filling her chest. She had kept herself from telling this story for so long, it was hard to break through the walls she'd placed around herself. Around this. But if anyone was going to believe her, it was Lachlan. Maybe he could even help her make sense of what had happened, help her understand the betrayal she'd endured from what she had considered a friend.

"One day, when I was on my way to visit her, a group of kids followed me," Emma said. "They were just bullies from my school, looking to make trouble. I was so scared,

I ran to my secret place. I thought I'd be safe there. But I didn't think things through."

She shook her head. "They were so close, one of them grabbed the back of my shirt just as I crossed the threshold. I shoved her off of me. When she fell, she crushed some of the herbs."

A wave of energy rippled through the shield surrounding her. She looked up at Lachlan to see his brow furrowed, his lips pulled in a deep frown. His chest was still, as if he held his breath, his attention so intent on her, it was a palpable thing. His concern broke the last wall within her. She said the words she hadn't uttered to anyone since shortly after the incident—after the adults in her life had failed her by not believing in her.

"She changed," Emma said. "Junebug... She turned into this horrible *thing*. This little monster with clawed hands and feet and sharp teeth—God, she had so many teeth. I was utterly terrified. So was the other girl. We both screamed and tried to get away, but we just ended up making it worse, trampling more plants. We tripped and were holding onto each other, and Junebug was stalking toward us with this look in her eyes like she knew we were afraid, and she was okay with it. Like she wanted us to be afraid. Wanted *me* to be afraid."

Emma's voice broke. Lachlan reached out and took her hand in his. She gripped it tight, drawing strength from him.

"I told her that she was supposed to be my friend," Emma said. "I begged her to let us go. She just screamed at us, this horrible noise. The next thing I knew, we were falling up into the sky, as if gravity had gone completely crazy. We landed on the sidewalk just outside where the alley entrance had been, but there was only a brick wall. We fell hard—hard enough to get hurt. I jumped up and ran home as fast as I could and slammed the door shut behind me."

Emma wiped at her eyes again. "I tried to tell my grandparents what had happened, but they thought I was in shock. It turned out, I had sprained my wrist and nearly dislocated my shoulder. They took me to the hospital, and the other girl was there. She had a broken ankle. I found out later that she hadn't said anything up to that point, but when she saw me, she said that I had climbed a tree and had purposefully dropped down on her while she was riding her bike, and that's how we both ended up hurt."

Another ripple passed through the energy surrounding her. She could feel Lachlan's rage, even though he was holding himself completely still. Emma hurried through the rest of it, hating this part even more than how much Junebug had frightened her.

"I don't think anyone believed I had fallen out of a tree on purpose, but the doctors said that I had suffered a trauma from the fall and come up with the story to make myself feel better. My parents never let me stay at my grandparents again. They put me in counseling, but I learned really quickly what to say—and what not to say—to be done with it."

The tears welling in her eyes spilled over. "But I knew. I knew that what I had seen was real. So I started researching everything I could on fairies. I wanted to understand what had happened. It wasn't even about how Junebug changed physically. I needed to know how she could scare me so badly. How she could *hurt* me. How could she do that to two little girls? Especially to one who was supposed to be her friend?"

"So you read Grimm." Lachlan's voice was tight.

"I read a lot of things," she said. "But the Grimm brothers were the ones who made the most sense. They told me fairies were capricious and tricksters. That they would fool you for their own amusement. Believing that was the only way I could make sense of what had happened at the time. Then I grew up, and the memory became more like a dream."

"And then you met me."

She smiled at him, some of her sadness seeming to lift. "And then I met you."

# Chapter Ten

The hair on the back of Lachlan's neck was standing straight up. His muscles were tight enough that it was almost painful. He wanted to do something to fix this, but Emma's pain was so far in the past.

"Most of the Fae don't understand human morality," Lachlan said. "It's alien to them."

Her lips tightened, her expression hardening. He hurried on, wanting her to know he wasn't trying to make excuses. He needed her to know that he was on her side.

"Some understand it fine and make the choice to spread pain and chaos wherever they go," he said.

Her eyes narrowed, but she didn't seem quite as guarded. At least she was listening to him.

"This garden you described sounds like it's either a pocket of Faerie in the mortal realm or the garden of an extremely powerful witch," he said. "Either way, the space would be marked with their symbol—and guarded by one of their protectors."

"You think Junebug was protecting the garden."

"It would make sense. She didn't become aggressive

until you damaged the plants."

"I was a child," Emma snapped.

"I understand that. But Junebug is… what Junebug is."

"A pooka."

"Yes, I think so. She's probably under a *gaes* that forces her to protect that site."

"A magical compulsion."

He warmed a bit at her knowledge. Her research may have hardened her against the Fae, but it had been sound. It was just incomplete.

"I don't think she meant to hurt you or that other little girl," he said. "She might have even been trying to protect you."

"Excuse me?" Emma angled her head, her eyes heating with anger.

"Pookas are relatively harmless Fae. They don't have much power. She shouldn't have been able to *gate* you out of the garden at all."

"*Gate?*"

"It's a form of transportation spell we use. Most Fae require a doorway that they can link from one place or even realm to another, and they have to be fairly high in the courts to do so. I'm honestly stunned that she managed it."

She shouldn't have been able to. With what Lachlan had learned from his short time with Emma, he was beginning to understand the true power that mortals held over the Fae. Even a pooka could boost their magic incredibly not by bonding with a mortal, but by caring for one. His heart sank as he realized that he didn't need Emma to fall in love with him for his powers to rise enough to balance those of the Yuletide Fae for the moment. He only had to fall in love with her.

*As I already have…*

"We got hurt," Emma said.

"Because she couldn't control her power. She just wanted you to be safe, and it manifested in an unexpected way."

"No." Emma's expression hardened, the walls she had built inside her mind once again stacking themselves brick by brick.

"Many Fae are capricious and dangerous," he said. "We aren't. The courts of the Wheel of the Year are tied in with nature. Nature is capricious enough. To maintain the balance, we can't be so mercurial. Yes, there is danger among the Fae. However, there is also beauty and wonder. You said that place held magic for you. You can feel that magic again."

For a moment, he thought he saw a wistfulness in her expression. Her lips parted, and she leaned closer. She might not be ready to give herself over to him, but maybe he could show her that she could at least embrace the role that had been given to her.

"Even if you don't fall in love with me," he began,

"even if you don't want us to be married, think for a moment about what you're trying so hard to give up. Everything you've told me about, all the wonders of being human that you've described, I'm experiencing them. And I know you're still feeling them, too, even though you're one of us now."

She shook her head, her lips tightening into a line again. What could he say to help her understand the infinite possibilities before her?

"You don't have to give up who you were because of who you've become," he said. "It's all still part of you."

"A fairy will say anything to get what they want."

She still didn't trust him. Not one bit. Her fear was all-consuming. She would never be happy as a member of the Fae. Never truly be happy with him. And he realized suddenly that he would never be happy with her because of that. He didn't want to be with someone who didn't love him the way he loved her. He didn't want to take that chance away from either of them—to love and be loved in return. And most of all, he wanted her to be happy. Even if it was with someone else.

"I think I understand now." Lachlan felt his heart harden, like bark growing over a wound. New growth would follow. It always did. That didn't mean he wouldn't grieve the loss of everything they could have had together, everything they could have been.

The open doorway from the kitchen to the hall

beckoned to him. His power flowed easily from his feet along the hardwood floor and up through the molding. Emma must have sensed it, because she turned, her eyes wide as she saw the light emanating from the portal he had created.

Leaving didn't feel right. It never would. The scales between them weren't balanced. But perhaps he could find a way to fix that. He adjusted the portal's destination, then headed toward the archway.

"What are you doing?" she asked.

"I'm giving you what you want. Your freedom."

"Wa—"

Her words were cut off as he stepped through the golden energy spanning the doorway, appearing on a porch. He looked back at the orange brick arch behind him, tempted to go back to hear what she had to say, wondering if maybe she would follow. He lingered for a moment, then dropped the spell when she didn't appear.

This was for the best. His kingdom needed a queen who could give her heart to them. That was a key component of what was needed to balance the Wheel of the Year once more. He was sure of it. He could keep things going for long enough to find another queen.

*Keep telling yourself that.*

He headed into the yard beyond the porch, letting his Fae senses guide him. The mortal world faded to muted grays, shimmers of color letting him know where the Fae had touched this realm. A flash of green began his trail. He followed it to a brick wall that glowed with a verdant light, thick with magic.

This was the place where his fate had been sealed. He was standing on the sidewalk where Emma had fallen as a child. Where the pooka's spell had gone wrong—or rather, not quite right. Junebug had probably saved Emma's life, as well as the other little girl's. The Fae didn't take well to trespassers.

Reaching out, he traced his fingertips across the brick surface, letting the witch beyond know of his presence. The bricks glowed brighter, then swiveled in place, curling inwards to create a doorway. Lachlan stepped through, unsure of who he would encounter beyond, but needing to know more.

The garden was just as Emma had described it. The lion's head fountain on the wall let out a stream of liquid filled with sparkling light, rich with magic. A wealth of herbs surrounded him, cobblestone paths winding through them and making a circular pattern around a tree at the center of the space. Thick blossoms of purple and lavender weighed down its branches and filled the air with a sweet scent.

Several stone benches curved beneath the tree, one of which was occupied. He could see the barest glimpse of a woman sitting with her back to him, her long black hair cascading down her back. She ran her hand over the empty space next to her in invitation.

Lachlan took a deep breath and let it out slowly. He was not looking forward to this. Witches weren't always aligned with any of the Courts. That made them wild cards. They only answered to the forces of nature. At least he had his link with the Wheel of the Year going for him. He strode forward until he stood before her.

She was as beautiful as he'd expected. Dark eyes, pale skin, full curves. She smiled and leaned forward, making her ample breasts push against the dark green fabric of her dress. Lachlan wouldn't even have noticed the tactic before meeting Emma. Now, he understood the appeal of physical affection much better. But he was only interested in sharing himself with Emma. He only wanted her.

"Well, well," the witch said. "What could bring the Oak King himself to my little garden?"

"It's just Lachlan when I'm in the mortal realm."

"Lachlan."

His name on her lips sent a zing through him. That shouldn't have happened. It wasn't his truename, but it was the only name Emma had called him. Did that lend it power? He would have to reinforce his protective spells, just in case. The last thing he wanted was to create some sort of bond with this person.

"Then you may call me Rose," she said.

"Rose." He chuckled. It was a brilliant name to give to others, especially seeing her affinity for plants. Beautiful and potentially dangerous. A plant with built-in defenses. "I suppose you have thorns."

"We all do." She smiled more deeply.

"I'm looking for something."

"Oh?" Rose patted the spot next to her again.

Lachlan didn't wish to offend her, so he sat. He also didn't want to remain there any longer than necessary, so he said, "A pooka."

She flinched ever so slightly, her eyes narrowing and her smile faltering. She quickly recovered, smiling even more brightly as she leaned closer, hooking her arm in his elbow. Her magic trickled over him, much too reminiscent of Emma's hands exploring him earlier. He sent out a surge of power, just a small one, but enough to let Rose know he was aware of what she was doing and it was unwelcome. Her smile became a bit strained, but she went on as if nothing had happened.

"A pooka?" she said. "What use would you have for one of those?"

"Curiosity," he said, choosing his words carefully. "I believe this pooka was involved in an event of interest to me. I'd like to meet her."

"'Her?' Most Fae call pookas 'it.'"

"I'm not most Fae."

"No, you aren't, are you?" She pursed her lips, head angled as she studied him. "I can't imagine a little guardian beast being involved in anything interesting enough to draw your attention."

"Humor me. I know she's here."

"Yes."

Rose tilted her head, looking over Lachlan's shoulder. He followed her line of sight to a small statue of an impish figure. Its arms were held above its head, a planter balanced in its clawed hands. Its face was contorted with strong emotion, its mouth wide and filled with sharp teeth. A tail was wrapped around one of its legs and its pointed ears and muzzle gave it only the vaguest catlike appearance. A surge of sympathy flowed out from him. The poor thing looked as if had been suffering when the spell was cast. Possibly even longer.

*Junebug.*

"What did she do to earn such a punishment?" he asked, keeping his voice calm and his expression impassive.

"Punishment?" Rose laughed. "No, that is necessity."

He stared at her, waiting for her to continue. It didn't take long.

"She was a loyal guardian for this space," Rose said. "But something drove her mad. I came back from a journey to find the garden partially destroyed. She was stuck in this form and in some sort of rage. I froze her to keep her from doing any more damage."

"Rage," Lachlan said. He looked back at Junebug, his heart tugging painfully as something beyond sympathy grew within it. It wasn't rage she was feeling. It was despair.

He didn't have to try to imagine what Junebug had gone through. He was going through something similar himself. The pooka had befriended Emma, had loved her. But the role Junebug was forced to assume had ruined everything. She had frightened Emma terribly and knew there was no fixing the damage that had been done to their trust. There was no way they could be together as things were. Something or someone had to change.

Lachlan's instincts had told him that he'd needed to come here to fully understand what had happened between himself and Emma. But there was more he needed to see. He stood, walking closer to the little pooka. With each step, his magic flooded out from him, more powerful than he could completely control. The herbs sprawled out of their beds, leaves plumping as they reached full maturity in moments, flower stalks shooting up and bursting open into full bloom.

He reached out to the plants to ask that they share their memories of this place. Shimmering light coated everything as the garden revealed what had happened. Emma sat on the bench near the witch. She was so young, Lachlan could barely see the woman she would grow into within her features. It was hard for him to believe that humans began this way, so helpless and small. She was reading a book to a gray cat who was nuzzled next to her.

Every time she paused to turn a page, she shared the pictures first, then gently stroked the animal. The cat angled her head into Emma's hand, fangs poking out from her lips as she smiled at the child next to her. Even without sound, Lachlan could feel the happy purr vibrating within her—the pooka.

The vision sped forward. Emma burst into the garden, another little girl right behind her, fisting Emma's shirt in her hand. The pooka jumped up from where she was sitting on the bench, eyes wide and pupils slitted. She looked down at her paws, saw how her claws were already extending, and started to back away from the pair. The children stumbled, falling into one of the herb beds and breaking the plants within.

Junebug shook her head, obviously fighting the transformation. But the *gaes* was too strong. Her body grew, her back cracking as her spine pulled her up into a hunched, bipedal stance. Her head rounded, eyes growing huge till they took up most of her face. Small, serrated teeth filled a mouth that now stretched from one side of her gray-furred face to the other. Her ears lengthened along with her arms.

The children had managed to get to their feet. The one who had chased Emma went to shove her, but then saw the pooka and froze. Emma turned to see what she was looking at and screamed.

The look on the pooka' s face... It would haunt

Lachlan for eternity. He could see her heart breaking, even as she continued to struggle against the spell that insisted she protect the witch's garden. Then the children tried to run.

Their feet tore into the soft soil, trampling and breaking more plants. Junebug let out a caterwaul, the magical scream invoking terror in the girls. She leapt down from the bench, her claws scraping against the stone as she charged them. Her arm was pulled back, claws fully extended to slash at them. Emma was saying something, but Lachlan couldn't hear in the memory. He could only see what happened. Emma grabbed the girl who had been chasing her and hugged her, turning so that she was between the girl and the pooka, her eyes clenched shut as she tried to protect her.

The pooka' s eyes widened. At the last second, she sheathed her claws instead and pushed Emma toward the magical doorway to the garden with a powerful blast of magic. Even after all these years, the residue of the energy was powerful enough to throw him out of the vision.

Junebug had sealed the history of the space as best she could, trying to protect Emma so that the witch's scrying spells wouldn't reveal who had actually damaged the garden. Lachlan's eyes watered from the brightness of it. He turned his back toward Rose and quickly wiped the moisture away. Calling on the energy of the plants in the garden, he wiped the memory clear so that no one else would be able to discover the truth of what had happened.

"Is everything alright?" Rose asked cautiously.

He could not show weakness. He could not show desire. And yet, he couldn't leave Junebug like this.

"Give me the pooka," he said. "And I will give you a boon."

Rose's eyes widened with a surprise she didn't bother trying to hide. Then the eyes narrowed, an unsettling smirk coming to Rose's lips. She stood and approached him, her hips swaying provocatively. She stopped quite close to him, her sultry gaze roving over his body.

"What sort of boon did you have in mind?" she said.

Instead of being intrigued, he was repulsed. An unpleasant shudder passed through him at the idea of being with someone else, anyone else other than Emma. He had to get over this—get over her—if he was ever to find another person he could love and rule over his Court with. But he couldn't bring himself to even consider that now.

He reached out and clasped Rose's hand. Her smirk deepened, and she arched a single thin eyebrow. The expression faded as he lifted her hand and held it between both of his, pushing some of his magic into it. The markings along his arms twitched, vines unfurling from his skin and curling around their hands. He watched as her sultry expression turned to one of shock, her smile widening in what looked like honest joy. His vines retreated back to rest against his skin and he released her.

"*Greenthumb*," he said. "That's worth a thousand plant holders, and that's all this pooka is to you anymore."

"Now you have me very curious. What could you possibly want with my little servant that's worth *this?*"

"*My* servant. And that knowledge is not part of the deal."

"I never agreed to a deal."

Lachlan stepped closer, so that she had to crane her neck to look up at him. He leaned down, knowing his frame wouldn't intimidate her, but his magic sure as hell would.

"I don't have to be nice," he said. "No one expects me to be. Dispel your *gaes*."

The words came out more bitter than he'd intended, but they were true. Among the Fae, kindness was not expected and seldom offered. He was sick of it. Even if Emma wasn't going to be at his side, he was going to make strides to change that.

After this exchange.

Rose knew that he could turn his 'boon' to *wither* easily. Any plant she touched or even breathed near would shrivel and die. From the looks of her garden, she was a green witch. Her power came from the plants. He had just made it exponentially more potent. She'd be a fool to push for more.

"I don't have to be nice, either," she said.

She waved an arm toward the pooka. A blast of dispelling magic came out from her. He felt the *gaes* drop, along with the spell of binding. Cracks formed along the pooka's skin, the stone sloughing off. The little creature crouched and let out a hiss. It's claws extended as it raced toward Lachlan.

"Junebug," he shouted.

The pooka's eyes widened as she skidded to a stop. She stared up at him, arms lax at her sides. Lachlan knelt before her and stretched out his hand. Junebug sniffed the air, testing his scent. Her eyes widened and she ran forward, grabbing his arm and running her nose along it. After his time with Emma, he had expected that her scent would be mingling with his.

Junebug looked up at him, her eyes shimmering with moisture. Lachlan nodded.

"Do you accept this as your truename?" he asked.

The pooka nodded, then crawled up his arm and perched on his shoulder as he stood. Rose glowered at them, her lips pulled in a frown.

"Who gave her a name?" she said.

"I did."

He doubted she believed him. He would have to keep an eye on this one. But for now, he had more important matters to tend to.

"Our business is done." Before she could say anything more, he let his power burst up from the ground, petals swirling around him as he summoned a vortex to take him away from this place. He stepped through the magical corridor into Crystal Creek park.

The trees had greened and the irises were blooming. In the distance, the trickling water of the park's namesake sounded. Lachlan reached up to Junebug and scratched behind her ear. She brushed her head against his and let out a little whine.

"I miss her, too," he said. "But I think I have an idea where at least one of us can be happy with her."

# Chapter Eleven

Emma paced the length of her living room. She was going to wear a path through the carpet at this rate. She had never thought she was the type of person who would wring her hands and fret, but here she was with fingers almost as sore as her heart.

Lachlan was gone. She had driven him away. And instead of that making her feel safe or happy, she was miserable and terrified—frightened in a way that was so much worse than any insubstantial fear of the Fae she had been blinded by before.

*What if he never comes back? What if I never see him again?*

Wasn't that what she wanted, though? To be free of her links to the Fae?

Lachlan was making her question everything she thought she knew about them. About herself even. She didn't want to be the kind of person who couldn't change their mind when presented with new evidence. She didn't want to let one experience cloud her judgment or define her perception of him. But that was just what she'd done.

And all because of what? One interaction with a fairy.

It wasn't even an isolated encounter. She and Junebug had had *one negative interaction*. Granted, it was a huge one, and Emma had been so young at the time it had been formative. She hadn't known how to process it. Any time she tried to get help with that, things only became worse. The adults she reached out to said there was something wrong with her, tried to convince her that she didn't know what she had seen. They hadn't intended to gaslight her, but that was exactly what they had done. So she had gone to the only source of support that she could find—books.

Books didn't judge her. They didn't tell her she needed therapy or imply that there was something wrong with her. In fact, the stories she read confirmed that she was right. She had needed to hear that so desperately as a child, needed support, validation and guidance. Now that she was an adult, she could make up her own mind, listen to her own heart. And her heart was yearning for Lachlan.

Energy was flowing out from her in a steady stream. She visualized it as a golden light that sank harmlessly into the earth. Except the longer he was gone, the more she worried that he would never come back. If she let her thoughts spiral, she had no idea what that would do. Hayden and Finn were busy preparing for the Feast of Beltane. Emma wasn't ready to call them for help… yet.

She needed air. She hurried out to the front porch. At least if she paced there, she could enjoy the spring breeze and maybe some sunshine. The pale blue boards creaked beneath her feet. Spring blossoms filled the air with their perfume. Closing her eyes, she took slow, deep breaths, calming herself. Lachlan was connected to her. She would have a chance to see him again. And when she did… She didn't know what she would do. Didn't know what she wanted.

*Another lie.*

Fine. She wanted *him*. She just didn't know how to get past her fear so that they could be together. A shiver flowed over her skin, the fine hairs standing on end. She opened her eyes to see one of her neighbors, Amelia, staring at Emma's front yard.

"Hi." Emma waved.

Amelia waved back. "You really have a magic touch."

"Why do you say that?" Emma asked warily.

"The beds… I walked by here this morning on my way to work, and I swear everything was just sprouting then." She laughed, then added, "I must have had too much ice cream at the parlor."

Emma's heartbeat picked up. She carefully looked over her yard, her mouth dropping open. Vines spilled over the sides of the beds, huge gourds ripening along them. The tomatoes were taller than their cages with plump red fruit weighing down their stems. All of her garden beds looked as if they had been growing for months.

"I'm jealous," Amelia said. "It's like it's already summer for them. I must have been daydreaming not to notice how far along they are. Whatever you're using for fertilizer is amazing."

"Yeah. Fertilizer."

It had to be her magic. Emma had to be more careful.

"Have a good evening," Amelia said, her voice cheerful and bright.

"You, too." Emma waved, then leaned against the post next to the steps, staring at the plants.

Movement at the edge of her fence caught her eye. She looked up to see Lachlan standing just outside the gate, staring at her.

Her heart pounded hard, as if it was trying to escape her chest and fly to him. Her mouth went dry, her skin prickling with the need to feel his hands on her. So many things welled up in her that she wanted to say, but she couldn't find the words.

Lachlan opened the gate that led to her yard, then looked down, smiling at something she couldn't see. A small gray cat ran around his feet, then darted down the path. It rocketed up the steps, straight for Emma, mewling plaintively as it wove in and out around her legs.

"Junebug?" she whispered.

The cat sat back with her paws in the air, not touching Emma but staring into her eyes, and let out a long, wailing meow.

"It's okay," Lachlan said, his voice gentle. He stood at the foot of the stairs, keeping his distance. "She was under a *gaes* to protect the garden. She fought against it to keep you safe. I've never seen anything like it. In any case, she's free from it now."

Emma couldn't breathe, couldn't move. She didn't know what to do or how to react.

"This is what she is now," Lachlan said. "It'll be permanent after Beltane."

Emma finally found her voice. "What are you talking about?"

"Junebug is bound to this form. She can't change into the shape that frightened you, and she can't use any magic."

An odd anger rose within Emma. "I didn't ask you to do that."

"No, Junebug did."

"I don't understand."

"She thinks the only way for you to feel safe with her is if she becomes a normal cat," Lachlan said.

That did not sit well with Emma. "But she *isn't* a normal cat. She's a pooka. You can't just change her into something else."

"I can and I will. If only all of us had the luxury…"

"Luxury? You don't get to decide—"

"I didn't," he said, his tone sharper. "She did. It's her choice."

"I…"

Emma stared down at Junebug. She was still on her

haunches, paws clasped in front of her chest as if begging for something. Begging to be with Emma? For things to be as they were before?

That could never be. Emma had grown up. She was a different person than the naive girl who idealized magic as a child. She knew things now that she couldn't unlearn.

*Maybe I can learn something new.*

"She loves you," Lachlan said, his voice gentle again. "And she's sorry that you were swept up in something that hurt you. Something I very much understand."

Was he only talking about the second part or the first? The way her heart beat even faster, she knew which she wished was the truth. She hadn't thought fairies were capable of love. But if Junebug was willing to give up being a pooka, if she wanted to become a cat just so that she could be with Emma... Junebug's willingness to change was one of the greatest loves that Emma had ever experienced. However, it was something Emma absolutely could not let Junebug do.

Though her hands were shaking, Emma knelt down and opened her arms. The little cat leapt into them. Emma caught her up against her chest, burying her face in Junebug's soft fur. Junebug rubbed her face against Emma's, purring louder than Emma had ever heard a cat purr before.

"Oh, Junebug," she whispered. "I missed you, too."

"So, you'll accept her?"

There was a rough edge to Lachlan's voice that made Emma look up at him. He was staring past her, not quite looking at her directly. She wished he would meet her eyes, that he would rush up the stairs the way Junebug had, and sweep her into his arms.

"I will," Emma said.

He let out a little breath and nodded, glancing away from the pair. She wanted to tell him that she accepted him, too. That neither of them had to change to be with her. Before she could speak, he quickly went on.

"It will be done at the Feast of Beltane," Lachlan said. "When I retrieve the magic of the Wheel of the Year and free you from all of this."

"But—"

A breeze picked up, filled with petals. She shielded her eyes with one arm, cuddling Junebug close with the other. The gust swept past her, swirling so forcefully that she could barely keep her feet. As quickly as it had begun, it vanished, and with it Lachlan.

She ran down the steps, turning in a circle, hoping she would see him somewhere. But he was gone.

"This isn't right. None of this is right." She hugged Junebug closer and shook her head, tears streaming down her cheeks. Junebug stretched her neck so that she could lick Emma's face. Her little body trembled in Emma's arms as if she was frightened.

"You don't have to do this for me," Emma said. "This

isn't right."

Junebug shook her head, then let out a soft meow.

"I mean it."

The pooka reached out and gently brushed Emma's cheek with a paw, then meowed again.

Was this really the monster who had traumatized Emma so badly against the Fae? Junebug was being as sweet as Emma remembered. They had spent so much time together like this—most of their time. Emma had been too quick to discount their history after that final encounter. Had that terrible experience really all been due to a spell and totally outside of Junebug's control?

The thought had never occurred to Emma. The only information she could find about fairies told her that they were capricious and did whatever they wanted just because it was in their nature. A nature that did not include love. If Emma had been able to find someone who understood such things, someone who would listen to her with an open mind instead of berating her for letting her imagination get the better of her, she might have been able to see another possibility. One where it was just a set of unfortunate circumstances.

Her heart sank. She should have had more faith in her friend.

Lachlan had called being able to change a luxury. Did that mean he wanted to change for Emma? Would he become human for her if he could? Did she even want that?

She had already been changed. She was a member of the Fae now. When it had happened, she hadn't wanted it. But after meeting Lachlan and getting to know him, after seeing this incredible gesture and feeling the love that Junebug was sharing with her…

Emma *had changed*. A deeper change than one brought on by any fairy's magic.

Shaking her head, she wiped her cheeks dry and stood straighter. "I'm going to make it right."

# Chapter Twelve

The Feast of Beltane came more quickly than Lachlan had expected. He stood wearing his pale green suit, wanting nothing more than to get this done. At the same time, he wanted the event to last as long as possible. It was probably the last time he'd ever see Emma. How did mortals deal with such powerful conflicting emotions?

Strangely, Finn was nowhere to be seen, though his work was evident everywhere. Lachlan was once more in the banquet hall where they had held the Feast of Ostara. He stood on a raised platform at the far end of the room, almost in the exact spot where Emma had been made the Queen of the Springtime Fae when the Holly King infused her with half of the magic of the Wheel of the Year.

Lilac trees had grown into the wood paneling of the room, merging with the structure of the building itself. Their branches flowed along the ceiling, covering it in a carpet of green leaves. Magic coursed through the floors, the walls, the ceiling, even the crystal of the chandelier hanging above him.

Hayden had accidentally unleashed her own power on Ostara while trying to protect her friend. At the time,

Lachlan had been dumbfounded at the strength of her magic. Now, he completely understood.

When you loved someone, anything was possible. If only Emma loved him, too.

"My liege."

Lachlan turned to see Finn standing behind him. Finn bowed low, one hand over his chest, then stood.

"I wondered when you were going to show up," Lachlan said.

"There's been a lot to attend to."

Lachlan nodded. "It'll be easier for you once Hayden has control of her magic and can help."

Finn's lips fluttered into a brief smirk. That was odd. Lachlan had never seen such an expression from him before.

"She's made great strides, my king."

"Lachlan. We're in the mortal realm."

"Right. Lachlan."

"I don't know why you wanted to have the feast here," Lachlan said. "The Feast of Beltane is for our court only. It's supposed to take place in our realm."

"About that… The actual Feast of Beltane is taking place in our realm for those in our court, as usual. This is a somewhat different celebration."

Lachlan turned as a glowing white portal opened behind him. A wintery blast of arctic air swept past him as the Yuletide Court stepped into the room. First Lord Snow and his mate, who was ironically named Spring. The huge man was the personification of his name, wearing a formal white uniform with rows of gold buttons running in two diagonal lines across his massive chest. The red trim around his collar matched the red glow from his eyes.

Lady Spring had her arm hooked with his. She wore a golden dress that seemed to capture the rays of the sun, its sparkling light gleaming within the citrine gems that studded the combs in her blonde hair. The pair smiled at him, Snow bowing and Spring curtseying before they headed toward the table they had occupied during the Feast of Ostara.

Another couple followed, this pair both dressed all in white. Both had golden eyes that glowed with magic. The man had dark hair and the woman bright red, each of them wearing a white fur cap. The White Stag and the White Doe, now the Lord and Lady of the North Wind. They wore slacks, with form-fitting jackets with two rows of gold buttons running vertically along their fronts. Both bowed toward him, then followed after Lord Snow and Lady Spring.

Finally, the Winter Queen stepped through, dressed in a shimmering gown that was such a light blue, it was almost colorless. She wore her crown, the platinum spikes rising around her pale blonde hair reminiscent of a star. The man at her side wore a suit of bright red with a single row of gold buttons running up his jacket and a black belt with a shining gold buckle. Though his mouth was obscured by his full white beard, Lachlan could see that Lord Kringle was smiling by the way his eyes crinkled at the corners. The Winter Queen inclined her head slightly in Lachlan's direction before a broad smile brightened her face.

What the hell were they so happy about? And why were they dressed in their Fae attire instead of dressing for the mortal realm? Lachlan's heart began to pound as a feeling of unease grew within him.

They made their way to their table while another portal opened just as theirs closed. This one was bright orange, its heat driving away the chill from the Yuletide Court. The rich song of cicadas echoed in the banquet hall as two men stepped through, their visages as disgruntled as those of the Yuletide Fae's had been happy. Both men were tall, with dark brown hair and malachite-green eyes. They wore dark green tunics over eggshell-white shirts with loose sleeves and brown hunting leathers tucked into riding boots.

*Lords Verdant and Game…*

"Please tell me Beast knows that the Huntsman is coming to the Feast of Beltane this year," Lachlan murmured to Finn.

The Lord of Summer Game and the Lord of Awakening Beasts, Finn's counterpart in Lachlan's court, had been rivals for as long as the Wheel of the Year had been turning. Beast considered hunting for sport outside of the cycles of nature and considered the Huntsman—Lord Game—his sworn enemy. The Huntsman only ever seemed amused by Beast's rage.

"They both know to behave," Finn murmured back.

A woman stepped through the portal behind them, dressed much the same, aside from the red cloak that was fastened at one shoulder and draped behind her. Her red hair was plaited into braids, some piled upon her head and some cascading down her back. Her emerald eyes sparked with malice as she glared at Lachlan, openly seething. She stepped forward as their portal closed, then turned and strode toward their table.

Lachlan nodded toward her while whispering, "Can you tell me why the Court of the Summer Fae all look like they want to rip my head off?"

A final portal opened before Finn could respond. At least by now Lachlan wasn't surprised by it. Its light was a deep purple with streaks of black. Another set of men stepped through, both tall and lean, with hair dark as a night sky. Black leather armor encased their forms, the chest plates emblazoned with a holly leaf in silver, the symbol of the Holly King. Lords Change and Solace looked profoundly uneasy as they glanced around the banquet hall. They bowed deeply toward Lachlan, then stepped aside as the Holly King emerged.

Lachlan wasn't sure what he expected, but it wasn't this. The Holly King was also dressed as if for battle, though he'd been wise enough not to come to the feast armed. His armor was more ornate than that of his Lords, with bits of obsidian metal worked throughout. A silver holly leaf held a dark purple cloak in place at his right shoulder. His lime-green hair was pulled back with a tie and his features were drawn in barely contained fury. He glared up at Lachlan from beneath a furrowed brow. The trio headed toward their table as their portal snapped shut behind them.

Lachlan angled his body so no one in the room could see his face, then leaned closer to Finn and muttered in a low tone, "You need to tell me what the hell is going on right now."

Finn actually had the gall to smile. He reached up and rested his hands on Lachlan's shoulders and gave them a squeeze. What in the realms was going on? Finn was never so familiar with Lachlan—with anyone, aside from Hayden. Were they overthrowing him? Lachlan couldn't believe Finn would do such a thing, but he couldn't think of a single reason that all of the highest members of the courts of the Wheel of the Year would be at the Feast of Beltane.

The double doors at the end of the room swung open. Lachlan wheeled around, ready for anything. At least, he thought he had been. Nothing could have prepared him for what he saw.

Beast entered the chamber with Hayden on his arm.

And he was wearing a suit. A full suit.

Lachlan had never seen the Lord of Awakening Beasts wearing so many clothes. He still wore his leather pants, but also wore a leather vest over a linen shirt that was tucked into them. The sleeves were rolled up past his forearms and the shirt was only laced up to his collarbones. He still looked abjectly miserable, his lip curled up in what had to be a perpetual growl. He scanned the room, his eyebrows flying up when he saw the Huntsman. Hayden made a visible effort to hold Beast back and murmured something. He flashed his teeth, which only made the Huntsman smile. Hayden murmured something else, and Beast settled down.

"She certainly has come a long way in a short time," Lachlan said.

"You have no idea."

Hayden was wearing a gorgeous lavender dress embroidered with spring flowers and studded with amethysts and peridots. She was the only one in the room smiling more broadly than the members of the Yuletide Court. When she and Beast reached the center of the room, he released Hayden's arm and stalked over to the last empty table, throwing himself into a chair while he glowered at the Huntsman.

Lachlan's attention returned to Hayden. She clasped her hands together and curtsied low. What was she up to?

"My king." She rose and said, "I was not prepared to

welcome you properly at the Feast of Ostara, but hope to make up for that now."

She lifted her arms, and as she did, the lilacs above began to move, their branches creaking as thick clusters of pale purple flowers burst into bloom, their sweet fragrance filling the air. The flowers began to glow. Little wisps of light floated down from them, hovering in the air and adding a gentle illumination to the banquet hall. Their light caught in the crystals of the chandelier, casting rainbows on the ceiling and walls. It was beautiful, but not as beautiful as the next sight.

Hayden stepped aside as a woman appeared in the doorway at the far end of the hall. She wore a white gown that trailed behind her and a veil covered her face. Diamonds and crystals were interspersed throughout an embroidered pattern of vines so intricate it had to have been made through magic. She held a bouquet of spring flowers—daffodils, irises, and tulips in every color.

Lachlan's heart pounded, his mind spinning with thoughts that were almost incomprehensible. Had Finn and Hayden already found him another bride? They wouldn't have. They knew better than most that Lachlan's queen had to be someone he could love and who could love him. He hadn't had a chance to move past Emma. He knew he needed to move on. And yet... Part of him wondered, hoped, didn't dare to wish, that this woman gliding toward him might be her.

"Finn..." Lachlan felt a crackle of warning in the name, his control of his own magic slipping. The lights glowed brighter, a tremor passing through the room as the lilacs spread further throughout the structure.

"It's okay," Finn whispered. "Trust me, Lachlan. It really is okay."

But for that to be the case...

The woman walked up the stairs, Hayden following, and paused in front of him. His hands were shaking as he reached out to lift the veil to reveal Emma's lovely face. She stood before him, a huge smile gracing her features and tears glittering in her eyes. Lachlan's breath rushed out of him even as an enormous energy flooded through his body.

"Emma," he whispered.

"I'm here," she said, and laughed.

"You don't have to do this."

"I know." Her smile faded and she stepped closer. "I *want* to do this. I want to be with you, Lachlan. Forever."

He grabbed her arms and pulled her close, pressing his lips to hers in a crushing kiss. This had to be real. It had to be, because he couldn't stand it if it were otherwise. She dropped her bouquet and wrapped her arms around his neck, kissing him back with just as much passion. Her magic flowed through him and his through her, as it was meant to be. As it would always be.

"Um, guys..." Hayden said.

They pulled back from the kiss as the floorboards beneath them groaned. Sinewy forsythia pushed through the minute gaps between the wood, merging with them in some cases and pushing them aside in others. Bright yellow flowers burst out from their branches. More flowers popped into view among their roots, clusters of crocuses, daffodils, tulips, and irises dotting the room and turning it into a springtime paradise.

Lachlan turned back to Emma and said, "Are you sure?"

"I've never been more certain of anything in my life." She angled her head to the side and said, "I just need one thing from you."

"Anything."

She smiled and turned back toward the door, calling out, "Junebug."

The little gray cat scampered into the room, darting between the flowers as she made her way to them. Even she had a lace collar around her neck that looked a bit like a cape. She stopped at Emma's feet, crouching low and wiggling her bottom.

"Don't you even think of running up this dress with those claws," Emma said. The cat mewed plaintively, and Emma smiled, kneeling down to pick her up. "You need to undo what you did to Junebug. She's been under spells long enough."

"But she said—"

"She said she wanted to be with me. She doesn't have to change what she is for that to happen."

Lachlan smiled, then reached out and swept his hand over Junebug's head, pulling his magic from her as he did. She gave a little shudder, then looked over at Emma. She nodded, and a moment later, Junebug shifted into her pooka form, though a much less toothy version. Once more Junebug turned her focus to Emma, her body stiff with worry. Emma smiled and hugged her tighter.

"Don't you have something for Lachlan as well?" Emma encouraged.

The pooka smiled and reached into her collar, pulling out two rings. Emma set her down, then took the rings and straightened.

"I didn't have a choice when I stood here before," Emma said. "But I do now. And I choose you." She lifted his hand and slid a large ring of pale gold, channel set with peridot, onto his ring finger, then handed him a smaller ring in a similar, if much more delicate motif, with a diamond at its center.

Lachlan could barely find his voice. He nodded, then grasped her hand and slid the ring onto her ring finger.

"I choose you as well."

Emma smiled, then reached up and threw her arms around his neck, kissing him again. Though the emotion swelling through him was just as great, there was a peacefulness to it now that tempered his power. They broke off the kiss and turned toward the room, taking in looks that were encouraging from some and what Lachlan was now certain were envious from others.

"I present the Queen of the Springtime Fae," Lachlan said.

Everyone in the Court of the Yuletide Fae rose with applause, those who had once been mortal cheering. The other courts stood more slowly, clapping grudgingly.

"We all must work to restore the balance of the Wheel of the Year," Lachlan said. "Together, I believe it is possible. We stand ready to assist the Courts as best we can."

While the Yuletide Fae merely nodded, the members of the other courts looked confused or even offended. Emma stepped closer, hooking her arm into Lachlan's.

"I think what he means to say is, we look forward to coming to all of your weddings soon."

A mix of scoffs and laughter rose at that. The Summer Queen openly sneered, still as angry as ever. She rose from her seat and summoned a portal in one graceful movement, stalking through it, Lord Verdant right behind her. Lord Game cast a salute to Beast before following. Once their portal closed, the Yuletide Fae opened theirs as well. They each bowed or nodded in Lachlan and Emma's direction before leaving. The moment the Yuletide portal closed, the Holly King summoned his own, scowling as he strode toward it.

"Wait," Lachlan called out.

The Holly King turned and stared at him.

"Our offer isn't hollow," Lachlan said. "We know how to balance the power of the Wheel of the Year now. We can help."

"I don't need your help," the Holly King said.

Lachlan shrugged. "Then know you have our thanks."

The Holly King narrowed his eyes, his lip curling up in disgust, then he turned and stepped through the portal. Lord Solace followed, but Lord Change lingered for a moment. He bowed low to Lachlan and Emma, then hurried through the portal. It snapped shut behind him.

"Well, that was something," Emma said.

"It certainly was," Finn agreed.

Hayden started hopping up and down. "Do I know how to throw an event or what? And it is so much easier with magic."

"Maybe let's give them a moment." Finn hooked her arm in his and led her from the room.

Beast stood and said, "Finally."

He tore his vest and shirt off, tossing them aside. As he passed near them, he made a clicking noise. Junebug's ears perked up and she ran to him, scurrying up his leg to perch on his shoulder. They followed after Finn and Hayden, leaving Lachlan and Emma alone.

Lachlan lifted his left hand, holding Emma's so he could see their rings together. They had to have been crafted by magic. Her dress, the room, all of it was done with a tool she had rejected so recently.

"There was certainly a lot of magic involved in this," Lachlan said.

"The best kind. Love." She stepped closer, squeezing his hand tight. "I don't know how it happened so quickly or how it's already so strong, but I love you, Lachlan."

He had never heard more beautiful words. A rush of power flowed through him, spilling out into the room and making more flowers bloom. She smiled as she noticed them, leaning into his chest.

He pulled her close and said, "I love you, too."

Emma smiled up at him. "Then this is our very own fairy tale. And one I'm sure will have a very happy ending."

"It will have a happy everything," he said. "For there is no greater magic than *us*."

"I couldn't agree more."

He bent his head to hers and sealed the promise of their joyful future with a kiss, the balance of spring restored.

# Epilogue

*How dare he. How dare they all?*

The Summer Queen charged into her Great Hall, lightning crackling through the windows high above as her rage swept through her realm. Water streaked the stained glass portraits of fields bursting with crops and horsemen riding on hunts through the forest. Her footsteps echoed from the stone, grating on her already frayed nerves. She swung her cloak aside as she turned and sat on her throne, seething.

One of her servants approached cautiously, her head bent so low that the queen couldn't see the woman's face. She set a goblet of wine near at hand and quickly retreated. As if the Summer Queen could stand libations of any sort at the moment. She tapped her fingers on the arm of her throne, trying to develop a strategy to deal with this colossal change.

It had seemed an anomaly when the Winter Queen had taken up with a mortal—one that was fixed for a time when they had fallen out. But now they were together again and her Fairy Lords had found mortal mates of their own. Mortal mates that somehow granted them extraordinary levels of magical power.

The Oak King had taken a mortal queen, as had one of his Lords. The Summer Queen had felt his Court's enhanced energy during their Beltane ceremony. No doubt, Lord Beast would soon follow suit, though she couldn't imagine a mortal woman strong enough to tame him. That one ran wild.

*He so reminds me of another…*

Lightning flashed through the windows, casting strange shadows in the hall. A crack of thunder that shook the stone walls of her castle quickly followed.

Mortal mates. All mortal mates. Was that the only way to grow her power? To find some human man to take to her bed? Their mortal mates were part of the Fae now, no matter how they had begun their existence. Much as another that she had known…

With a growl that turned to a shout, the Summer Queen knocked the goblet from her throne. The burgundy liquid arced through the air, splattering the floor as the goblet clattered against the stone. She rubbed at her forehead, trying to ease the dull ache that was settling behind her eyes. Her ears were ringing. No, not ringing… Hissing.

She sat up straighter, staring at the spilled wine as wisps of vapor rose from it. Clutching the arms of her throne tightly, she drew on her magic. The wine began to bubble, then finally burst into flame. The fire danced in the air, suspended for a few moments as it took on different shapes. The rune Kenaz, then Mannaz, and finally Thurisaz.

*Knowledge, memory, chaos.*

The words popped into her mind, her magic interpreting the meaning of the runes as it consumed the wine. Wine that had been imbued with a powerful spell.

"Verdant," she shouted. "Game."

Both men appeared at the entrance to the Hall more quickly than she had expected. Almost as if they'd already been en route. A deep foreboding took root within her chest. It grew stronger as the men neared.

"The servant who was just here," the Summer Queen said. "Where is she?"

"We ordered the servants not to disturb you," Verdant said. "We thought you would want some time to collect your thoughts."

"Well, someone was here," she said. "Someone who meant me ill."

"We know, my queen." Verdant cast a glance at Game, who studiously avoided her gaze.

"What is it?" she demanded.

"My queen," Verdant began, but his voice trailed off. He looked to Game again, this time, his eyes beseeching.

In a low, level voice, Game said, "It's about your daughter..."

—

Thank you so much for reading *The Oak King!* Writing this trilogy as spring blooms around my home has helped bring me an even greater appreciation for the beauty of this season. It's been so fun to imagine all the characters in Crystal Hollow enjoying their own spring. I've loved spending this time with them. So much that I'm not quite done! Read on for a sneak peek at a special bonus story for the *Court of the Springtime Fae* trilogy, *Lord Beast*! You didn't think I would leave him out of the 'Happy Ever Afters,' did you?

# Lord Beast

## Court of the Springtime Fae
Interlude

## Chapter One

"Cages secured, alarm on, bag on shoulder, door locked." Ashley went through her nightly checklist as she slid her key into the lock of the door, visualizing each task to make sure she had actually remembered it. When she had moved to Crystal Hollow, she'd thought she would be less busy in the small town. Little did she know how many pets lived there—and that she would be the only veterinarian in town. She had already hired two assistants from the college to help, but was thinking of finding a third.

"That's a tomorrow problem," she murmured. "The more immediate problem is me standing here talking to myself as if I'm with my patients while my key won't turn in the bleeping lock."

She let her head fall back and sighed, glancing up past the red brick building to the starry sky above. Her frustration eased. The townsfolk made an effort to keep light pollution to a minimum, so the small lamp next to the back door wasn't enough to wash out all the stars. It was barely enough to help her see her way to her car on most nights, but a huge full moon hung above her. Silverly light bathed the nearest dogwoods as she glanced around, making their white petals glow brightly.

It was absolutely lovely, but for some reason, a shiver passed over her as she stared at them, the hair on the back of her neck standing on end. Her heartbeat picked up suddenly, a cool spring breeze playing over her skin. Her clinic was in a newer building built on the outskirts of the small town, which meant it was right next to deep forest.

She was usually glad they had preserved so much of the lush woods that filled the area, but as she stared more intently at the trees a few yards away, she suddenly wished they weren't quite so close. At least her car was nearby as well. She wished she knew what had set off the primal warning center of her brain, though.

*Be careful what you wish for…*

A shadow beneath one of the trees shifted closer. Her heart beat even faster. The door wasn't locked yet. She could always dart back inside. For the moment, she held completely still. The shadow inched closer, becoming paler as it entered the light. Her eyes widened in disbelief, her brain struggling to make sense of what she was seeing.

This was not the proper ecosystem for capybaras and Crystal Hollow didn't have a zoo for one to escape from. Besides, it's ears were much too long, its fur softer and a lighter brown. Whatever this was, it was as big as a capybara. No, as big as a golden retriever, but its narrowed eyes and oddly intimidating stance made her think this guy wasn't nearly as friendly. It hopped a bit closer. Hopped.

A rabbit. It had to be a rabbit.

*How is it so big and… gnarly looking? And why do I feel like it's stalking me?*

"Flemish giant rabbit," she said, even though this particular specimen was much bigger than anything she'd heard of on record. "The largest domesticated breed." Something clicked in her mind. "Domesticated… You must be somebody's pet."

It rose on its haunches, its head nearly on the same level as hers, and sniffed the air. Granted, she was pretty short, but still. It held its right front paw close to its chest, as if protecting it.

"Oh no, are you hurt?"

It dropped to all fours and turned back to the forest. With a final glance at her over its shoulder, it slowly limped back into the shadows.

"Crap. Wait... Please wait!" She jiggled her key and it finally turned. As soon as the door was locked, she dropped her keys in her pocket, straightened her medical bag on her shoulder, and hurried after the beast of a rabbit.

The darkness in the forest would have been complete if it weren't for the full moon above. Even that wouldn't have helped if spring was much further along. The trees were covered in small leaves, their lime green faded to a silvery hue. The light that slipped between them illuminated the forest floor, deepening the shadows but also highlighting the twigs and stones littering the ground in a soft gray. She was careful not to twist her ankle as she followed the sound of the rabbit just ahead.

"Hey, bunny," she called. "Maybe wait up a minute? I mean, you came to me for help. It would be a lot easier if you actually stopped and let me help you." She stumbled a bit over a particularly rough section of ground. "Please? Pretty please?"

The ground beneath her gave way and she slid down a short hill. She barely managed to catch herself on the edge of a cliff, scrambling for purchase on its edge.

"Shit, shit shit!" she yelled, her voice getting higher and higher as the loose earth crumbled beneath her fingers.

She stabilized herself enough to glance around and saw that it wasn't a cliff but a large hole that she'd fallen into. She heard a thumping sound approaching. The rabbit, charging toward her, its fur shimmering with silver from the moon and its eyes glowing with a bright green light that trailed behind it.

"I'm dreaming. I'm dreaming," she chanted, as panic grew within her. "I have to be dreaming."

The rabbit bounded up right next to her, skidding to a stop at the edge of the hole. It's large feet dug into what was left of the soil, knocking it loose. With a scream, Ashley fell backward into darkness. The moon and stars quickly vanished, leaving her falling in an inky void. Her arms and legs flailed, her heart pounding as panic gripped her. If there wasn't water at the bottom of this hole, she was going to die. Even then, without handholds, she would drown. She sucked in a huge breath, hoping for the best—that there was water below and she could swim to a safe area.

Too much time passed. She took another breath and held it. This time, she counted as she fell. She reached fifty before she dared to take another breath. How deep was this hole? She looked down between her feet and saw a speck of light the same green as the rabbit's eyes.

Was this a dream? It felt much too real to be a dream.

But it also seemed utterly impossible. The giant rabbit. The endless fall. It was like a fairytale.

The light grew larger, closer. She clenched her eyes shut as a final scream escaped her. This was it. Whatever was going to happen, it was now. Her scream cut off abruptly as she landed on something soft. Somewhere in her mind, she knew that she should lie still as she assessed herself for injuries, but adrenaline took over. She bolted upright, her eyes flying open.

She was in a bed. A huge bed, with pale green curtains tied to dark cherrywood bedposts. The footboard was carved with an ornate forest scene, complete with spring flowers and woodland creatures. She twisted around to see that the headboard had a similar design, dominated by a huge oak tree at its center, its branches stretching above the fluffy pillows behind her. She looked up, but didn't see the long tunnel she expected. Instead, more of that pale green fabric stretched above her, providing a canopy for the bed.

"What the…"

A low growl rumbled out through the room, vibrating through her bones. Her hair stood on end once more, her heart speeding and her stomach tight. She gripped the strap to her medical bag and rose on her knees, staring around both to find the source of the noise and to try to figure out where she was. The walls beyond the curtains were made of an even darker wood, the paneling gleaming from the light of several lamps placed around the room—actual lamps, their wicks flickering within the glass surrounding them.

Her theory that this was a dream grew stronger. This room was like something out of a fantasy. She would probably wake up slumped over her desk with paperwork stuck to her face. Again.

Maybe she should pinch herself. But she wasn't done exploring whatever this was. Even if it was a dream, she wanted to know more about what her subconscious was trying to tell her. That she needed to rest more? She already knew that. If she had a bed this nice, she might spend more time in it.

Maybe she needed to pamper herself more? She would rather spend any theoretical free time she could scrounge up to find a date than take a spa day. It had been way too long since she'd enjoyed the company of a significant other. Something about spring always made her restless in that regard—probably the cycles of nature. Her DNA wanted her to find a mate, and all that creative and fertile energy floating around always messed with her.

Movement in the shadows near an enormous wardrobe caught her attention. Something was there. *Someone.*

Her mouth went dry, her voice shaking as she said, "Who's there?"

The growl grew louder and coalesced into a word. "Beast."

"Beast?" What kind of name was that? Oh right. It was a fantasy-dream name.

Her mind spun with stories she'd read as a little—and not-so-little girl. Princesses swept away by monstrous beings who were transformed by their love. Ashley had always been wary about the part where the woman changed the man. She was more a fan of two like souls finding each other or two people who truly understood each other bringing out the best in their partner. Still, as long as she was here, she might as well make the most of it.

"I can practically hear your mind working." Beast's gravely voice sent a shiver down her spine, a hint of laughter edging his words. "There is no sorting this out. You've fallen into a fairytale."

"Does that mean you're my Prince Charming?" she said, trying to keep her voice light.

He full-on growled. She caught two flashes of green light in the shadows where he stood. Were those his eyes? They glowed like the preternatural creature who had literally sent her down a rabbit hole.

"I am Beast," he said. "Not Charming."

"Well, I'll try not to hold that against you." She laughed, but he didn't join. The glowing embers of his eyes narrowed. "Because see, charming is an adjective, and if you're not charming, then some people would consider that unappealing. Hence me saying that I wouldn't hold it against you. To not be charming."

His eyes were the tiniest slits by the time she finished rambling. "Prince Charming is my counterpart," he said. "I am Lord Beast."

"*Lord* Beast. Okay then." She let out a nervous laugh. "I didn't realize I was in the presence of royalty. I'd bow, but I really... don't know how."

"It's a useless skill."

"Exactly," she agreed a bit too enthusiastically. He didn't say anything for long enough to make her uncomfortable. She fumbled for more to say. "So... are you going to do that whole 'dramatic reveal' thing where you slowly move forward so I can see your monstrous visage?"

He chuckled, the sound sending another frisson of pleasure through her. "If you wish."

Her heart was in her throat, eyes wide, her entire body leaning forward as the anticipation built within her. For a dream, it had been really good so far. She only hoped seeing him wouldn't twist everything into a nightmare.

He didn't move slowly, but strode out of the shadows confidently. Ashley wished the room was more brightly lit so that she could see him better. Not because he was monstrous, but just the opposite. He was the most gorgeous man she'd ever seen.

He stared at her with eyes that glowed bright green from beneath striking eyebrows that arched across his forehead like a robin's wings. His dark hair was pulled up in a top knot that seemed out of place with the robust beard that did nothing to obscure his strong jaw. He was huge—at least six feet tall—with broad shoulders and a chest she probably couldn't wrap her arms around. He wore dark leather pants, his feet bare and toes curling into the thick burgundy carpet.

A pale rose vest hugged his torso, showing off his perfect waist and thick hips. She snapped her eyes away from them as explicit images of what it might be like to wrap her legs around those hips assailed her. His shirt was a paler pink, unbuttoned at the top and with the sleeves rolled up past his elbows revealing corded forearms. She was rethinking all her associations with pink.

*Even his collarbones are sexy.*

That rumbling growl of his picked up again, resonating through her in a vibration that went straight to her core. Her belly flooded with heat, her skin prickling as she imagined his hands on her.

Maybe it was one of *those* kind of dreams. Staring at him, she wouldn't mind at all.

—

What an adventure we've been on! Exploring Crystal Hollow has been such a delight, and I'm thrilled you've come along with me as these mortal women find their powerful Fae mates. The Wheel of the Year isn't over. We still need to know how the Courts of the Summer and Autumn Fae are going to balance out the magic of their seasons. In the meantime, you can see how this all began with the ***Court of the Yuletide Fae*** trilogy!

I'd love to keep in touch. Join my newsletter at **cassandra-chandler.com/newsletter** to hear about all the adventures happening in Cassland. And if you enjoyed this book, please consider leaving a review at your favorite book review site. Reviews are so important to authors. You can also help by spreading the word among your friends. I appreciate you so much!

Thank you for reading *The Oak King!*

Cassandra Chandler

# About the Author

USA Today Bestselling author Cassandra Chandler uses her vivid imagination to make the world more interesting, spawning the ideas she turns into her evocative Science Fiction Romances and enthralling Paranormal and Urban Fantasy Romances. Fast-paced and funny, lighthearted or filled with suspense, her stories will introduce you to characters you'll fall in love with and worlds you long to explore.